WESTE

FOLK
TALES

WESTERN ISLES
FOLK TALES

IAN STEPHEN

The History Press

Illustrated by Christine Morrison

First published 2014

The History Press
The Mill, Brimscombe Port
Stroud, Gloucestershire, GL5 2QG
www.thehistorypress.co.uk

Reprinted 2017

British Library Cataloguing in Publication Data.
A catalogue record for this book is available from the British Library.

ISBN 978 0 7524 9911 6

Typesetting and origination by The History Press
Printed in Great Britain

CONTENTS

Acknowledgements   9

Introduction   11

1   **BARRA HEAD TO ERISKAY**   **14**

The Secret of the Sailor   14

John's Leap   22

The Two Caves   27

The Cattle of Pabbay   32

The Tale of the Three-Toed Pot   35

The Black Tangle   39

How the Down was Shared   43

Donald and the Skull   46

The Cask in the Foc'sle   51

The Point where English was Spoken   55

Words of Help   58

2   **SOUTH UIST**   **61**

The Crop-Headed Freckled Lass   62

The Kingfish   67

Two Ravens   70

The Cooper's Beautiful Daughter		73
Asking for the Wind		75
3	**BENBECULA TO GRIMSAY**	**80**
	Out the West Side	81
	The Day of the Black Dog	84
	A Way of Taking Herring	87
	Threads of Three Colours	90
4	**NORTH UIST AND OUTLYING ISLANDS**	**92**
	The Beachcomber	93
	An Elopement	95
	Black John	99
	A Boat Race	102
	Holding Together	104
5	**HARRIS AND OUTLYING ISLANDS**	**108**
	The Cowhide	109
	Matters of Justice	111
	Anna Campbell	116
	A Crossing to Scarp	120
6	**LEWIS AND OUTLYING ISLANDS**	**124**
	WEST LEWIS	124
	An Endless Voyage	125
	Who Was Chasing Who?	128
	A Father and a Son	131
	The Tale of the Head of the Flounder	136
	A Transaction	139
	The Blind Woman of Barvas	141

EAST LEWIS   **143**

The Blue Men of the Stream   144

The Spoons of Horn   148

The Tooth of the Fairy Dog   152

An Apprentice Seaman   156

An Encounter   164

From Father and Mother   165

Smith's Shoe Shop   167

Looking Where You're Going   169

NORTH LEWIS   **171**

A Disappearance   172

The Two Brothers   174

A Fertile Island   177

A Note on the Sources   182

Appendix   188

ACKNOWLEDGEMENTS

The author wishes to acknowledge the continuing support of Creative Scotland, The Scottish Storytelling Centre, and the Highlands and Islands writers' support body, Emergents.

An outline for this work was first developed during a Creative Futures Residency, with Western Isles Libraries, developed and administered by Shetland Arts.

Two other residencies, in Orkney and Shetland, were instrumental in developing a method of producing written versions of oral stories. Thanks to Orkney Islands Council, Shetland Arts and Book Trust Scotland.

Direct assistance from a Traditional Arts Grant from Enterprise Music Scotland enabled the author to devote the time to research and develop much of the detail of the contents of this book.

The resources of the School of Scottish Studies have also been invaluable. Particular thanks to archivist Cathlin MacAulay.

ALBA | CHRUTHACHAIL

Shetland *arts*

N

Outer Hebrides

LEWIS

NORTH
MINCH

HARRIS

NORTH UIST

GAIRLOCH

ISLE OF SKYE

THE LITTLE
MINCH

BENBECULA

SOUTH UIST

BARRA

THE SEA
OF THE
HEBRIDES

INTRODUCTION

The idea of the Western Isles means different things to different people. For this book, it is the region from Barra Head to Butt of Lewis – the long chain of islands that comprises the Outer Hebrides. Investigating the range of traditional stories linked to this geography, it became obvious that the many stories rooted in offlying islands must also be represented, though sadly many of these landmasses no longer hold resident populations.

Since 1979, the Outer Hebrides has also been an administrative entity under Comhairle nan Eilean Siar – the Western Isles Council. Before that, there was a dividing line between Lewis to the north, as a part of Ross and Cromarty and Harris and the Southern Isles, all linked to Inverness-shire. This led to the astonishing but true situation where one twin was born on the island of Scarp in Harris (in one county) and the other was born in the neighbouring county after the mother was taken by boat and ambulance to hospital in Stornoway.

Some of the islands that lost their populations (usually in the twentieth century) are close inshore, like Taransay and Scarp (off Harris), or the chain of islands south of Barra like Mingulay, Sandray and Pabbay. And some lie out in open ocean, like Hirta (*Hiort*), the island in the St Kilda archipelago, about 40 miles west of the Sound of Harris, inhabited until 1930. The culture of Heisker or the Monach Islands, west of North Uist, is less well known but this is a very prolific source of tales. There are also stories linked to annual gannet-hunting expeditions to the bare rock of Sula Sgeir, 40 miles north-north-east of the Butt of Lewis, and others set on North Rona, a further 11 miles north-east, once a fertile farm which supported a few families.

The author came to storytelling through family background and mentors at sea and by the harbour. In this part of the world a conversation often becomes a story, once the engine is shut down and lines are cast, on the drift or at anchor. There seems to be a particular name and a tradition for every species of fish caught and every stage of that fish's growth.

What exactly is a story? The conclusion is surely that there is the finest of lines between a person's memory of a recorded historical event and a story. Then there are the huge number of premonition accounts and strange sightings told as a person's memory of an actual experience. There are also remembered twists of eloquent wit. Examples of all of these are included, as well as tales that could easily fit into a worldwide pattern of folk-tale types. Stories remembered from different 'ceilidh-houses' exemplify how the contemporary and the timeless bounce off each other at an informal gathering.

The selected stories are retold in the author's voice. This has sometimes involved intuition, in navigating between different known versions of the same story, whether from oral or published sources. Place names and spellings of the names of people are in English versions throughout. The vast majority of these stories were originally told in the Gaelic language. Most of the oral recordings are in Gaelic and many of them can be heard at www.tobarandulchais.co.uk. Several generous friends have translated original sources and shared the cultural associations behind a phrase or tradition.

This book takes a mainly geographic rather than thematic approach, travelling south to north, as far as the outlying North Rona. However, the tradition of the mysteriously successful sailors who prospered on Berneray, south of Mingulay, implies a variation on a story also told in Homer's *Odyssey*, common all through the Western Isles but also told in both Orkney and Shetland. Many of the tales reoccur in different settings, and certainly myths relating to fish and fowl are very similar to others told throughout the world. In contrast, many other tales relate to a named point of land.

Ian Stephen was born in Stornoway in 1955. He studied Education, English and Drama at Aberdeen. It was there that he began to perform stories and poems in public and met Stanley Robertson, the storyteller. At Keith Folk Festival he met both Hamish Henderson and David Campbell. Both became friends and both encouraged him to continue bringing the stories, from his own Hebridean background, to a wider audience.

After winning the much-coveted storytelling cup at Kinross Festival, Ian went on to meet many other storytellers, including Belle and Sheila Stewart and Betsy Whyte. At the Tales of Martinmas Festival, run by Bob Pegg (author of *Highland Folk Tales*, in this series) and the folklorist Marie MacArthur, Ian experienced kitchen ceilidhs with Duncan Williamson, Alec John Williamson and Essie Stewart. He has often performed with musicians and singers. At Tales of Martinmas, he alternated stories along a sea-route with Mary Smith's Gaelic sea-songs. He also developed performances for the Harris Arts Festival with the late Ishbel MacAskill.

Ian still lives in Stornoway but travels widely to perform both poems and stories, and lead workshops. He is a regular guest at the Edinburgh International Storytelling Festival and the Without Borders Festival in Olomouc, Czech Republic. He has been a guest at Cape Clear Island Storytelling Festival as well as at several events in Northern Ireland. In 2014 he represented Scotland in Canada as part of the Scottish Poetry Library's Commonwealth Poets United project.

Ian's cross-arts collaboration with the visual artist Christine Morrison was a central part of the 2013–14 Voyage show commissioned by the Edinburgh International Storytelling Festival and performed at Rathlin Sound Maritime Festival and Settle Stories. The continuing work can be followed at www.stephenmorrison.org

1

Barra Head to Eriskay

MINGULAY

BERNERAY

BARRA
HEAD

The Secret of the Sailor

You could never keep a vessel moored there, through the winter. You come out of the tide-rips, off Barra Head, looking up to a strong, squat lighthouse. It grows from cropped grass that's still rich and green. Then you enter the kyles to the north of Berneray, from east or west till you find some shelter, off the stone jetty. You need to clear out of there, though, if the wind blows from either east or west. In fact, when you look at it, I don't know how any sailors managed to run a boat from Berneray, even in the better months of the year. I suppose they were only lying at anchor there when the weather was settled.

Shepherd Duncan married into a Barra family and was given land on Berneray because there was little enough left elsewhere. Their bairns, when they came, had to be sailed over to Mingulay to be schooled but they did well enough. Every bite that family took and every stitch they wore came from the land or the sea. They had no need of the merchant's credit and so they prospered. The crops grew well on the land that had been fallow for long enough and the seas were still rich with cod and ling, which could be salted and dried for export. So it was not only a matter of feeding a strapping family. The Duncans were engaged in trade and their luck with the land was more than matched with their luck at sea.

The shepherd and his lads, in season, went from the line fishing to the herring. Soon they were talking about sailing up the west side of the Outer Hebrides as far as Heisker, where the lobsters are known to be at their best. As the years went on, the family moved from working small, open skiffs to running a proper trader, with a white topsail. They were daring and they'd sail that trader to Ireland or they'd sail her up to Lewis. Or anywhere there was a market for their produce or their catch. She moved with the seasonal fishing and she was never, to my knowledge, caught out. But I've heard they came close to it once.

That year there was an exceptionally good summer at Heisker. They'd caught more than their share of all the lobsters to be had and they'd done good trade, getting them over to Uist to market. But it was a better breeze to go north than to head south, for home. And the Heisker lads, who had given them a good help all summer, were very keen to see their relations on Lewis. It was the least they could do to give them a lift up the road in their fine, seaworthy craft.

The topsail was flying, white above the tan mainsail, and the wind was where every sailor wants it, there on your shoulder. Their stout vessel made good way, over the waves, with a following sea. And this time there was no work to be done on the way. The boat was going like a collie through heather and they were all wearing that daft grin sailors get. It was a soldier's wind – the strength and direction that would get the voyage done fastest.

Soon they were moored in the lee of Mealasta island, off the south-west coast of Lewis. They could take their small punt ashore till they saw what was what. The Heisker boys had relations not so far away. 'Boys', by the way, is a flexible word. Some of them might have been well into their sixties. They were made welcome. Everyone was invited ashore, with one fellow left to watch the anchor. Conditions were ideal. Islavig and Brenish are fairly remote places and folk were very happy to see their relatives from the islands. The crew were in the fortunate position of being able to carry the stories from Heisker and from all the islands south of Barra.

Gallons of tea were consumed along with mountains of bannocks. As long as they didn't run out of yarns and gossip, they were welcome for as long as they wanted. Their skipper was beginning to get twitchy, thinking that their luck with the fair weather couldn't last forever. But one of the younger lads kept persuading him to stay for one more night. The very first day they were ashore, he'd set eyes on a dark-haired girl. He said something offhand to his relation, something like, 'That's a strange looking one.' And the reply from his old aunt was, 'Strange looking or no. You watch she doesn't get a hold of you.'

Sure enough, the young fellow was drawn every night to the house where the dark-haired girl would take her place by the fire. It was the done thing to be going round the houses, sharing the news. But that crewman kept going to sit across from that girl.

At last the skipper put his foot down. 'Come on now, lads. We've a long way home and we'll need to get the boat into safe harbour in Barra before the gales set in. The breeze is favourable.'

So it was, when they carried their small skiff back down the beach. So it was, as they set sail and hauled the anchor. But the minute they were moving, clear of the island, the breeze turned on them. It was soon right on the nose and blowing strong. The lads looked to their skipper and weren't surprised when he said, 'We can't fight this, boys. We'll need to get her back into shelter.'

They managed that. And again, the boat was well secured. Most of them rowed ashore while they waited to see what the wind would do.

But they weren't alone on the beach. An old woman was working away at her knitting. She walked while she did that but she was still watching them closely.

'You're having a bit of trouble getting home, boys.'

'Aye, the wind's turned half a circle. She's blowing hard against us.'

'I'm not surprised,' says the woman, 'seeing the company some of yous are keeping.' And she gave that certain young lad a pretty withering look. 'Which one of you is the skipper?'

He took a step forward.

'You don't sound like a Heisker man nor a Barra man neither,' she said, 'but maybe I can help you just the same. Now would you happen to have a bit of tobacco or snuff left from your travels?'

The skipper shared out the last of his pouch even though he was indeed running low after all that time away from Heisker. 'How can you help us?' he asked.

'Well,' she said, 'it's not natural, the wind shifting as sudden as that. There's someone here doesn't want to see that fellow sail away from her clutches. That's why the wind shifted.'

'What can we do about that?' the skipper asked.

'That dark one isn't the only woman who can do something about the wind,' the old woman said, chewing away happily.

Now this is every sailor's dream. You are at the mercy of the wind at sea and there's no sailing boat ever invented that can head right into the teeth of a hard breeze. Even the lads fell silent.

'How can you do that?'

'I'll give you something that will help you on your voyage if you use it the way I'll tell you.'

She dug into her skirts and produced a short length of thin cordage. When they looked at it closely they could see the oily old cord had three knots in it. But none of them were knots any of the boys had seen before, from Barra Head to Heisker. They said so.

'Well you're seeing them now, skipper, and this is what you'll do. I'll tell you for sure, when you set out again, that breeze will shift back against you. When that happens you can let the first knot go.' She pointed it out.

'What will happen then?'

'You'll get a fair breeze, from over your shoulder. That fine boat of yours will eat up the miles, with no effort at all.'

'Grand, but what do we need the second one for?'

'You don't need it at all but I know what you men are like. You'll want her to go faster. If you think the boat and yourselves can take it you can let that second one go – that one in the middle.'

'What about the third?'

'No, no, you have to promise me right now, you won't even look at that third knot. You have no need of that but the others won't work without it.'

'Well, why would we need it if the other two will work as you say?'

'Oh, they'll work all right.'

But some of the boys thought their skipper had been a bit generous with his tobacco, for an old bit of string.

When the breeze settled back, they launched their craft again and got a wave from the old woman, still chewing away. But they had only just hoisted the gaff when they felt, on the back of their necks, that change in the wind again. One of them only looked glad at the thought of returning to the beach. The others urged their skipper to let that first knot go.

It didn't happen at once. But they could feel it on their cheekbones, the wind veering round till it was blowing from the north, but just a shade of east in it, coming off the land and not too strong. That would do them.

So it did and they were all, but one, very happy to be heading homeward now. Some had only to make it to Heisker and the other lads would help take her on to safe haven in Barra. They weren't many minutes before someone said, 'You know, I think she could take a bit more.'

'Aye,' the skipper said, 'I believe she could.' He fingered the cord in his hand, making sure he knew which end was which. Then he let go the second knot. If she was going well before, she was at the maximum now. It was absolutely to the limit of what she could carry under full cloth. Every rope was singing and every plank was creaking. The nails were shimmering but nothing gave way.

Soon there was a long straight wake behind them and spray coming over them. There was strong light too and that was catching the breaking spray. They were licking the salt off their lips and lost for words, for a change, as the miles flew by. One after the other, the islands were left behind, off to port, Scarp and Taransay and the outlying Glorigs. That couldn't be Coppay already, but it was. None of them had sailed like that before and even the reluctant fellow was starting to smile.

So it wasn't long before Heisker was in sight. The helmsman had his eye on his mark and they were almost in the lee of it when, of course, someone said, 'What about that third one?'

'No, boys,' their skipper said, of course. 'You heard me promise that old soul. We're going just fine.'

Did they give up? One after another they had a go at their wise skipper.

One of the Heisker men said, 'I thought we had a chief of Berneray, the skipper chosen by the Duncans of Barra Head, in charge. But he's a man who's scared of a poor old woman from Lewis.'

That did it. The skipper fingered the last knot. He took a glance. They were now coming into a lee. They'd gone the deep route, round Shillay, a small island to the west of the group. They were now sailing into more sheltered water. 'It can do no harm now,' he said, plucking at the cord with his fingers.

That was fine until the helmsman looked behind. You could see the shadow of fear cross his face. The first of three impossible waves took a grip of them and they were surfing out of control. The second one nearly had her over but the mast came down and the sail with it. There was water everywhere. When the third one hit, their fingers were all frozen to the gunnels. Just as well, because the force of the wind took the boat out clear of the water. They couldn't see a thing for all the hail and sleet, driving at them. But they could feel it all right. She was hurtling back in the other direction.

When the storm-driven rain cleared for a moment, they made out the high shape of an island passing by. It was an island they'd seen not very long before. Their vessel came down with a shudder, grounding at the beach. It was a beach they knew all too well. And here too was a woman they'd met before. She was shouting at them, higher than the wind. But they all knew what she was saying, all right.

'I told yous not to untie that third knot.'

I suppose that's where the story ends. The boys got away with it by the skin of their teeth. They were all handy enough with their repairs. And just maybe their skipper sacrificed the very last of his tobacco to regain the favours of the woman who could tie the right knots. That would certainly suggest that the Heisker lads and the Barra lads all got home all right. It might also explain the continuing good fortunes and successful trade of the family who made such a good living on the Isle of Berneray.

References
This is a story told the length of the Long Island (Barra Head to Butt of Lewis) and beyond. It hints at how a sailor might get more than his fair share of favourable breeze. John MacPherson (Coddy) makes a link between Barra and Coll and the Clyde with a similar tale and here on Lewis our telling navigates a route down the Atlantic side of the chain of islands, to Heisker or Monachs. But in a recorded discussion with a John MacNeil, also of Barra, John MacPherson describes a line of respected mariners and crofters who made a good living for themselves on Berneray. That is the most southerly island in our chain, but trade with Heisker, which lies to the west

of North Uist, is also mentioned. So it seemed a small step to splice these strands of story together.

My first memory of this tale is from conversations with both Norman Malcolm MacDonald and Francis (Frank) Thompson, part of the last days of Stornoway's Italian café culture. I sadly miss both these gentlemen. Frank's publications are too numerous to list in full but I'd recommend *The Supernatural Highlands* (first published in 1976 and reissued by Luath Press, Edinburgh,1997). Frank's poems are less well-known but they are wide in scope and finely made. Norman is the author of many plays, as well as the innovative novel *Calum Tod* and a small number of minimalist poems. The lore of the sailing vessel is prominent in his later novel, *Portrona* (Birlinn, Edinburgh, 2000), which gathers many strands from his drama. His play *Anna Caimbeul*, broadcast on Radio 3 as well as widely performed, was described by himself as 'the first Japanese Noh play in Gaelic.'

Notable versions of the tale are in John MacPherson's *Tales from Barra*, edited by John Lorne Campbell (Birlinn, Edinburgh, 1992, p. 141). See also Donald MacLellan's strong version, with some additional details, in A.J. Bruford and D.A. MacDonald, *Scottish Traditional Tales* (Polygon, Edinburgh, 1994, p. 391).

Traditions relating to Shepherd Duncan of Barra Head from transcriptions of John MacNeil and John MacPerson are in John Lorne Campbell, *A Very Civil People* (Birlinn, Edinburgh, 2000, p. 115). A Shetland version of the three knots is also included in Bruford and MacDonald's *Scottish Traditional Tales*. John Gibson Lockhart describes a visit to Stromness, Orkney with Sir Walter Scott. The account includes details of a woman who sells the winds for a sixpence. Common Orcadian versions (heard from Tom Muir, author of *Orkney Folk Tales*, in this series) have coloured threads rather than knots and the boat arriving back where it departed from, unlike most Western Isles versions where it is wrecked or driven high on dry land.

The story invites comparison with book 10 of *The Odyssey* by Homer. I suggest the rugged translation of Robert Fagles.

John's Leap

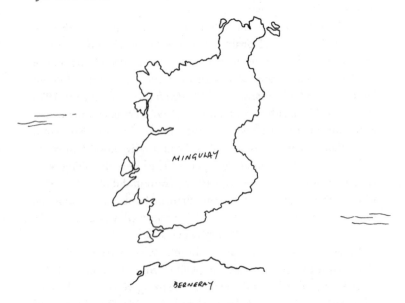

MINGULAY

BERNERAY

The west side of Barra is no place to be at sea in a gale. Once, a Spanish ship was caught out on this lee shore. They would come to these prolific seas to take cod and ling. The catch was split and salted and packed, to take home. It takes a long time to tack a vessel like that through the wind and her canvas was soon in tatters. There was no doubt she would be driven ashore. A line of folk was soon stretched along the rocks. They watched her ground. The wind was storm force and they knew that even a solid oak ship could not last long. It was heart-rending, watching the shadows of men clinging to the masts. No one could swim through that surf without assistance.

A strong rope ashore – that would be their only chance. The strongest and fittest man on the beach was one John MacNeil, a son of the chief. He coiled a long length of light line and weighted it with a securely tied stone. He chose his pebble with care, heavy enough to carry the line against the full force of the wind and light enough to fly far. The shoreward end was attached to fathoms and fathoms of heavier rope, all joined and coiled so it would run true.

It was an exceptional throw and John's line was seen to pass over the decks. The men on the shore felt a weight come on it and sure enough their heavy line was pulled out to be secured round the stump of a mast of the stricken ship. Most of the sailors were dragged through the surf on that line. They came shivering and gasping to the care of the Barra folk. But the stone at the end of the light line had struck the temple of one of the men on deck – a youth, really. Who should that be but the son of the skipper.

That Spanish man looked for revenge for the loss of his son. He blamed their hard fate on the Barra folk, gathered at the shore. He thought they were waiting for plunder. It was a harsh law then and a death demanded another death. He tried to insist that MacNeil should condemn his own son John, as the man who had thrown the stone. At this, the Barra folk rallied round their own and refused any further hospitality to the shipwrecked sailors. The Spaniards took passage across the Sound to South Uist. This was the territory of Clanranald, hardly a friend to MacNeil. When the rival chief heard the story and the claim against young John, he saw it was in his own interests to take the Spanish captain's side. He was seeking favour with the powers in Edinburgh. His neighbour, MacNeil, laird of Barra, had already lost that favour. There was a fair chance Clanranald would gain lands for his loyalty in pursuing a claim against any of that family.

John MacNeil knew that sooner or later the power of a navy could not be resisted, not even by the independent Barra people. He also wanted to spare his father's folk a ruinous war. So he went into exile. He didn't have to go far. The west side of Mingulay, the island to the south of theirs, is as rugged a territory as you can imagine. The cliffs fall away into boiling seas and skerries. Few would dare to navigate these waters. The only landing place was the steep shelving beach on the east side. If a ship anchored off that, you'd spot it easily, from the high ground of the island. There would be time to hide.

There's a steep cliff called Biolacreag on the west side. Across from it, there's a detached pinnacle. It was too steep for even a skilled fowler like John or the folk of Mingulay to descend and ascend on ropes. But John knew he could have a secure hiding place, if he could bring himself to make the leap.

He would have to make the short approach, then make sure his leading foot hit the edge at just the right place, when his run was at full power. There was a scattering of tufts of thrift and then he was in the air. His hands were out to grasp anything that could stop him from sliding back. They did find a hold and his feet were secure on the pinnacle. There was a shorter run, in making the leap back to Mingulay. But one thing made the return easier. If he did not leap he would starve.

Once he'd made that jump once, he knew he could do it again, both ways, if he had to. No one would think a man could be so desperate. In fact there is not another soul known to have made that jump before or since. Now there was a hiding place where a fugitive could evade his hunters.

So he did, but Clanranald did not give up easily in his attempts to deliver John to Edinburgh for the supposed crime. The MacNeils were seen as pirates and John was seen as the man with a claim on his head. As a lawyer will advise you, justice is for the next world. In this one, the law is all about probabilities and the way the evidence is presented.

There was another fugitive of a kind on Barra then. He was from Kintail, maybe an outcast from his own folk but he was given another chance. He was granted a piece of ground at Eoligary. Soon he was sent to Uist, to buy seed for the ground and seed potatoes to sow. Clanranald saw his chance. The Kintail man could have all the seed he could carry for nothing, and keep the silver, if he helped with one small matter.

Back in Mingulay, John, the exile, was a fine hand with a boat. He liked nothing better than to row to the rich fishing at the outlying reefs. He'd been chased once or twice by a heavy Clanranald boat but none could get near him nor navigate in the rocky shallows. John could thread his small craft through the tightest of gaps. The Kintail traitor stopped off at Mingulay, with a share of the seed. He said he wanted nothing more than to join John in his craft, to work the outlying reefs. John said that this was not the day for it. It was blowing hard from the north-west.

But he was a proud man. His seamanship was being challenged by the goading of the Kintail man, so he said he'd give it a try. The traitor had replaced the stout thole pins with weak ones of poor pine. They could not stand up to the strain. Sure enough, they were put to the test as the Clanranald vessel rounded an outlying point – it was known as the promontory of the thumb. The MacDonalds were rowing strongly. If they could capture this outlaw, the clan would be in favour with the king in Edinburgh.

'They won't get near us,' John said as he put his back into it. One by one the pins snapped like carrots. They were soon overhauled.

So, because of grudges and alliances, John MacNeil was taken to Edinburgh and charged with piracy. Some said that the Spanish ship was not the first to be wrecked on that coast. The testimony of the ordinary Spanish sailors who owed their lives to the Barra folk might have saved him. But these men were back in their own land or else at sea. So it was inevitable that John was sentenced to die.

There are further twists and turns in different versions of the tale. Some say he was reprieved for a few days, at the request of an influential woman who admired this strong man, but only till she'd tired of him. And, of course, the accounts from other islands, particularly that of Morrison of Lewis, portray the same John as a ruthless adventurer. There is no mention of his role in the rescue of fellow mariners.

It seems clear that he met a gruesome end, in that city. But how can we say now if John was a martyr or a murderer?

References

John Lorne Campbell, *A Very Civil People*, p. 113. See also Donald Morrison, *Traditions of the Western Isles* (Stornoway Public Library, 1975, from now on referred to as the Morrison manuscript):

> John MacNeil, brother to the then Proprietor of Barra, was a man of uncommon fortitude and, with his followers, he infested the seas of Barra for many years. So extensive were his piracies that he sometimes took trips with his galley to Ireland and sometimes to the Orkneys, plundering cattle and goods from both places. Notwithstanding the exertions of the surrounding clans MacNeil defied their efforts to arrest him for many years. His Majesty the King set a great reward upon his head and more than once sent a party of soldiers to apprehend him. But all these attempts were fruitless, so that many mariners ceased to navigate in Barra waters.
>
> Many grievous complaints were made to the king, who was at last so incensed that he made it up with the Captain of Clanranald, who was a man of great power and he undertook to capture the pirate or to die in the attempt.

The quote is from 'John MacNeil, the Pirate' (Morrison manuscript, p. 99). The very different accounts agree on the terrible form of execution. After being reprieved from being burned at the stake, the 'pirate' was placed in a barrel with spikes driven through and trundled down the hill at the city's edge. See also the Morrison manuscript, p. 62, 'The Tutor of Kintail [this could be an error – other sources refer to the *Traitor* of Kintail] and MacNeil of Barra'.

There are other stories of great leaps in the Morrison manuscript: 'The Leap of Allt' (p. 45) and 'Garry's Leap in Mull' (p. 335), which is similar to a Lewis story where a man humiliated by his chief takes a terrible revenge by leaping off a precipice holding the chief's son.

The trick to capture John at sea suggests comparison with Orkney traditions, retold as a Cain and Abel story set at sea, 'Befoor's Geo', in Walter Traill Dennison, *Orkney Tales and Sea Legends* (Orkney Press, 1995).

THE TWO CAVES

This time we'll put Morrison the cooper's account first. The men from Harris needed provisions. They left silver on a stone outside a quiet house on the island of Eigg. The man charged with buying provisions for the returning vessel placed the value of the sheep there, for the villagers to find. Then he carried that sheep on his shoulders, back to the shore. But he never reached the waiting boat. The men from Eigg were returning from their work and saw what they saw. They ran with knives drawn and did not pause to hear the desperate man's pleas. His fellow crew also knew there was no reasoning with men with their blood up and rowed swiftly clear, before hoisting sail for home.

When the folk of Eigg found the silver they knew the Harrismen would be back in force. They knew they could not challenge MacLeod's might so they made their preparations.

When the birlinn arrived, carrying a band of experienced fighters, well-armed, they found a deserted village. They raked the length and breadth of the island and found not a soul. They thought they had searched behind every rock that could conceal a human being. Someone said the people might have fled to Muck, the neighbouring island. So they pulled their ship out again but as they were about free of the shadow of the Sguirr, the shape of the high point of the island, the ship's lookout saw a movement on the high ground. So back they came.

This was early in the year and there was a light flurry of snow. The Harrismen were able to find a footprint here and there, left by the scout who had watched their brown sail hoisted and thought the folk of Eigg were now safe. The faint marks led to a small indent in the rock, up from the shore. They had searched a huge cave, a few yards along. But this appeared to be an entrance so narrow that even a hare would have to squeeze through it. They looked more closely and saw that the narrow entrance opened up to a huge concealed cave. And here were the shivering refugees from the village.

Some say an offer was made. 'Send out the men who murdered our kinsman and the rest can go free.'

If they did, the offer was refused. So branches and heather were taken and a fire was set at the mouth of that great cavern and all the generations of the place perished in there. Perhaps not all. I've heard it from Nan MacKinnon of Vatersay that one man came staggering out, coughing and retching, but alive. It took him a long time to take in enough breath so he could walk. When he did recover, his steps took him back to the site where a living village had been. It was desolation. The roofs were burnt. Amongst the smouldering stones, he heard a scraping, scratching noise. It came from a kist which had not been tumbled or burned.

The man was MacPhee. He opened the lid to find a boy curled up and shaking. He'd been too scared to go with the rest, to the cave. He held out his arms to the lad. 'I know whose son you were before. But you're my own son now. We'll look after each other.'

There was nothing left for them there. The first vessel that called in for provisions was from Barra. MacPhee found some stored meal for them and said they could have it in exchange for their safe passage.

'Well, you can pilot us out,' the Barra skipper said.

He just handed over the tiller and the lad helped with the steering as his new father pointed out the marks. 'I'd put in a reef now, boys. There's always a sweeping gust comes down at the point.' So they did. MacPhee and the boy were left at the tiller as they seemed to know what they were doing.

The wind grew stronger. MacPhee looked calm, still. That gave the boy confidence too. 'I think it's time for another reef, don't you think,' he suggested to the skipper. When it blew for all it was worth, MacPhee looked so easy there that the skipper judged it best to leave him where he was. At last the skipper and his new helmsman agreed they'd be better off without any cloth at all. They could run her on the bare poles. They could hardly see a thing but the man from Eigg knew where to point her. Soon the high ground of Muldoanich was in sight and they were nearly home to MacNeil's territory.

Their chief was glad to see his trading vessel had come through the gale. The skipper had a word in his ear.

'My men are not easily impressed,' said MacNeil, 'but they seem to think you know your way about the sea.'

'It's a thing I've always done.'

'Would you take work with me? That's not the only vessel under our command here. Will you take a boat to Mingulay? There are stores to bring in and the rent to collect.' Then he turned to the boy.

'Do you think they pay me in silver?' he asked.

The boy had hardly spoken. Now he said, 'Not in silver. Unless it's herrings.'

MacNeil was impressed with the answer. 'No, it's not fish that swim in the sea.'

'Is it birds that fly in the air?' the boy asked.

'It is indeed. The people of Mingulay pay their rents with barrels of salted fowl.'

Folk favour different meat in different places. In St Kilda they go over the cliffs for the fulmar. In the north of Lewis they sail out to take the young gannets from the rock. But in Mingulay it was the Manx shearwater.

It's not an easy approach. It looks like a fine sloping beach, free of reefs (and it is), but it's a steep one. The surf looks small enough but it sucks at your keel. The boy was up in the bows, ready to jump with the painter. He did that, wanting to prove himself useful. But then he handed it over to one of his father's crew and went ashore at a run. He was starting to come alive again.

As he was running, the men in the boat began to exchange looks. The houses of stone and turf were set deep into the green bank, the rise from the shore. You hardly saw them till you were close. There was no smoke coming from the chimneys. It was then they heard the boy's cries. Their new skipper was for leaping ashore but his men held him back.

Sure enough, the boy was shouting something about dead people. 'All of them dead.'

Once they heard these words the crew realised that some sort of plague or smallpox had hit Mingulay. The boy had been into a house.

They knew that MacPhee could not leave his adopted son. They took the hands of their skipper and tied them behind his back. Then they rowed, as the bowman shoved and the boat was afloat again. The boy tried to wade out but the surf overpowered him. They saw him regain the shore.

When the boat put in to Castlebay, MacNeil heard the full story. 'You can't blame your men,' he said. 'They did the best thing for all of us. Your boy could have carried that plague to Barra. We'll give it one month. Then you can take your pick of my ships and my men and return to Mingulay. If your boy lives, you can make a living for yourselves there. Mingulay will have your own name on it.'

A key was turned in a lock. They all knew MacPhee would have found some way to reach that island. The month passed. He was released.

'The same boat and the same crew will do me fine,' he said. He didn't waste a minute. They were away on the tide. He kept hold of the sheet himself, getting her moving, as well as she possibly could, using every bit of the breeze they had.

As they came close, his eye went to line up the top of the hill to take them into the beach. The rock he had in sight was quivering. It often seems like that, from the sea, lining up a mark. But this particular rock began to run down the hill.

His son knew he could do nothing for the folk of the village. He kept to the high ground. If you go there, you'll see where two slabs of rock once fell together. They form the most basic of natural shelters. He took silverweed from the ground and shellfish from the shore, to keep himself alive. So you could say that the lad who had lost nearly everything in one cave was saved by another.

The crew then gave the remains of these poor folk a decent burial. It would not be the only village in the Hebrides that would need renewal of its people. But there was no shortage of folk on neighbouring islands who needed the ground which had already been prepared by others.

The people prospered there for many a year. I'm sure that lad made a good life for himself, wherever he went, when he came of age. Or he might have found all he needed close to their new home. But they left their mark all right. It's there now on the map in the name of that high ground. Of course it's called MacPhee's Hill.

References

There are many recordings of Nan MacKinnon in the archive of the School of Scottish Studies. Several tales told by her are transcribed and translated in Bruford and MacDonald. The connection between the massacre on Eigg and the Mingulay plague story is told by Nan in a publication produced by the Barra Historical Society. But it is also suggested in the notes of contemporary folklore made by Father Allan MacDonald and reproduced, without full acknowledgement, in the publications of Ada Goodrich-Freer.

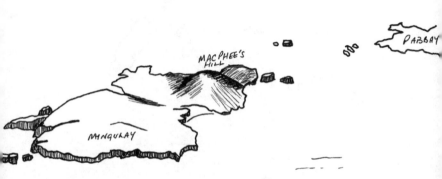

An account of the plague on Mingulay and the survival of the MacPhees was also recorded by Alexander Carmichael from a Roderick MacNeil.

The Morrison manuscript, p. 67, transcribes an account of the massacre on Eigg from a different perspective and I have used this version as the irony is poignant.

Neil Gunn, the novelist, also mentions the story of the massacre in his account of a 1937 voyage, *Off in a Boat*. Originally published by Faber and Faber, it is now back in print by House of Lochar, 1998.

THE CATTLE OF PABBAY

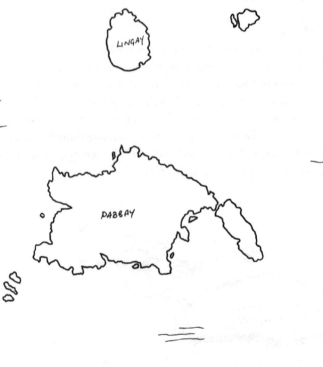

The houses on Pabbay, the island north of Mingulay, were no different from most of the houses throughout the Outer Hebrides at the time. People lived very close to their animals then. The barn was an extension of the house, made the same way, with thick walls and the same material in the thatch. Long and low, so the winds would sweep over humans and cattle alike. You also gained the warmth of the beasts. I suppose you grew used to the smell.

There was a man and wife who took over a croft on Pabbay. Ordinary people couldn't really buy houses or land then so it must have been given over to them by family, or maybe other folk had left or passed-on so there was a croft waiting for those who would work it. This couple were known to be very hard-working. They were sure to make the best of the Pabbay croft. So the stock was left with the ground and the walls. There was a cow, not the youngest of beasts, but she was known to produce the best of calves. She was distinctive and her good traits were passed on to her calves.

Years passed and the croft flourished, as much as any did in that part of the world. We're not blessed with good ground, to start with, though there's plenty of wrack on the shore to make it all the more rich.

As the years sped by, these people came to be considered well-off by the standards of the time and place. The quality of their beasts had something to do with this.

There came a time when the husband said that the old cow had really done her work. He was for selling her when they could still expect to get something for her. His wife was horrified at the idea.

'We will not sell her,' she said. But her husband did not give up. He was a very practical man and good at trading. He knew what it cost them in time and feeding stuff to keep that old cow. At last he said, 'Well, if we're not going to sell her we might as well get the meat off her. Now's the time, before the winter feeding starts.'

The strange thing is, this idea was easier for his wife to bear than the thought of selling that old cow and knowing she might not be so well looked after in her last years. So they talked on by the fire, about how much salt they would need and the basins and pails and the barrel that could keep the salt beef for the winter. Now that they'd decided, there was no point in delaying the job. Nobody is very keen on doing that deed so the husband said that he'd see to it the very next morning, before they changed their minds.

He rose even earlier than usual and left his wife in bed. He knew it would be hard on her to hear what was going on even if she wasn't outside to see it. But after he'd taken his tea, there was no sign of the cow in the byre, only a wide open door with a draught coming through it. Not only that, but the rest of the stock – the best of the beasts they'd kept for breeding – they were gone too.

He walked the length of the croft and found the gate at the end of the dykes open. He followed the hoof marks down to the machair and they led all the way to the shore. He must have covered every inch of Pabbay before he returned home to find his anxious wife standing in the byre and wondering what on earth was going on.

People lived and worked close together then. Before long, the neighbours were round. One of them had been awake in the night and seen a strange sight. He said there was a line of beasts, with their old cow at the head of it, walking down the croft, towards the sea.

Folk were scratching their heads until they thought to ask the oldest person amongst them. This fellow thought back and then he spoke.

'Your cow was on this croft when you came here yourselves,' he said. 'And all your stock, the black calves, came from her.'

Everyone nodded.

'We all wondered where that black cow came from. We now know she came from the sea. But something must have disturbed the old girl.'

'Only last night we were talking it over, how she'd had her day. How it was time to sharpen the knife.'

'Oh, well, she heard you then. She didn't hang around to wait for it. But when you lose a cow from the sea you lose all the stock that ever came from her. We won't see the cow nor any of her calves on Pabbay again.'

Neither they did.

References

From a recording of John MacPherson, 'The Coddy', transcribed and translated by John Lorne Campbell in *Tales From Barra* (Birlinn, Edinburgh, 1992)

It's interesting to compare it with the Welsh story of 'Physician's Point', where all the beasts given as a dowry from the Old Man of the Lake return to the water after the bargain is unintentionally broken. Also the tale of 'Llyn-y-Fan Fach'. There are many sources.

THE TALE OF THE THREE-TOED POT

I don't know how much you've heard about the fairy people. This part of the world they didn't have wings and they were not as small as all that. Some people said they were all that was left of an older people, the ones who occupied the land before stronger, new settlers came from Ireland and from Scandinavia. That would explain why the fairy people had no liking for iron. They could not bear to touch cold iron unless they were protected by the recitation of a charm.

There was a woman on Sandray who seemed to be able to get on with one of those folk. She called her 'a woman of peace', though her husband was never so sure about their visitor. She would come, most days, to borrow the three-toed pot. Every house had one of these, back then. It could stand on a low fire or you could hang it from a chain. The fire was in the middle of the house and the smoke just found its way up through a hole in the thatch.

Their understanding was like this. The small woman from under the hill would appear and ask to borrow the pot. The Sandray wife would say aye, she could, but first she'd need to say her piece:

A smith burns black rock
Cold iron warms with coal
His pot hungers for bones
And must come back whole.

Something in the wife's rhyme allowed the woman of peace to put her hand to the pot. She always kept the bargain and returned it before the end of the day. When it came back it would indeed contain some good bones for soup or even a picking of meat. So her husband never grumbled at their visitor.

But they couldn't find or make everything they needed on that small island. This day the wife said that stores were low and she'd need to get herself rowed across on the ferry to Castlebay. She'd soon be back with the basics they needed. But her man wasn't to forget to see to their visitor. She got him to repeat the rhyme and promise to say it before he handed over the pot.

So she was off and sure enough it wasn't long before he looked out from the open door to see the fairy woman approaching. But there was something strange about the way she moved along. She was not walking and not running. It was as if her feet were nearly off the ground and flickering shadows were coming from them. That man took fright and went back inside, pulling the door behind him.

Their visitor was none too happy. A deal was a deal and she'd always kept her side of the bargain. So she called out that she'd come to borrow the pot, as usual. The man said nothing. He just hid in his own house and wouldn't open the door to her. But she didn't give up that easily.

The three-toed pot was placed as usual in the middle of the floor. He saw it give a jolt and then another. At the third jump it was up in the air and out through the hole in the thatch. So that was that. He was not looking forward to his wife's arrival home, tired after her day, going for stores.

It didn't take her long to notice the loss.

'Is herself not back with the pot then?' she asked.

'That's the least of our worries.'

'What do you mean? Did you not say the rhyme as I told you?'

He had to admit that he had not. 'We shouldn't be dealing with that one anyway,' he said.

'I'll have to deal with her myself then,' his wife said. 'I can't even trust you to do the one thing I asked,' she said as she put her coat on. She was not willing to lose either the pot or the bargain which kept them in soup. She strode out of the house there and then. Out into the mouth of the night.

That woman knew exactly the place on the hill where the fairy woman lived. You could easily pass it by but there was a mound of earth, grassed-over. That gave away the spot. She just had to look for a stone that would roll aside or some such thing so she could find the entrance. That didn't take her long, either.

She peered in and could hardly make out a thing. There didn't seem to be anyone at home. There was just enough light to make out the shape of her pot, standing there in the middle. She took a step in and put her hand to it. It was heavy with the remnants of a good meal, bones and meat as usual.

Right then she heard a snore. It came from the shape of a small old man, hunched up, not far from the pot. She wasn't going to give up at that.

That woman had the heavy pot in her hand and was nearly back out into the light when it clanged against the stone at the entrance. The old fellow was awake in an instant. He saw her trying to get out with the pot swinging beside her and the remains of their dinner in it.

He shouted at her but it came out as his own line of verse:

Those in your house fell dumb.
So our dogs will be off their leash.
Woman from the dead side of the slope,
You'll meet the black and the fierce.

At that, he unleashed the two dogs which had been lying unnoticed at his feet. She was away like a shot from a gun. The dogs were snapping at her heels. She could never outrun them. But she threw a bone from the pot. One would stop for a moment to grab it and worry at it then she would run a bit and throw another. That way she kept them at bay till she was very nearly back at their own house. But she was down to the very last bone.

There was such a din from the howling of the fairy dogs that their own dogs came out to see what the fuss was about. The strong, fast collies soon put both the fierce one and the black one to flight.

She was still clutching her pot. She put it back in its place. A little gasp of triumph sneaked out as she caught her breath. Then her man had his arms around her. They were doing a little dance round their hearth, delighted to have their pot back.

They were never bothered by the fairy woman wanting to borrow things ever again. They always managed somehow to find something worth boiling up in the three-toed pot of iron.

References
J.F. Campbell, 'Sanntraigh', tale 26, in *Popular Tales of the West Highlands*, vol. 2, from Alexander MacDonald, Barra, 1859. Retold in George Douglas, *Scottish Fairy and Folk Tales* (A.L. Burt, New York, 1901).

See also recording from Calum Johnstone, Barra by D.A. MacDonald (Bruford and MacDonald, 67; see also notes). The Morrison manuscript also has several tales of chases by dogs from another world.

THE BLACK TANGLE

The whole length of the Outer Hebrides you'll hear stories of how the goodness of the milk could be stolen, leaving an unhappy cow and troubled people. Usually folk had no idea how it was done but they thought they could see the signs of it, something beyond bad luck.

There are very fertile strips, close to the shore on Vatersay. At that time there was a good head of milk cows kept on that small island. The beasts would be left to roam to find their grazing and often enough they were down on the beach. People were thinking maybe that's why the yield of the cows was down so much. They were spending too much time walking on sand rather than finding grass. This day there was a good head of them, along the shore.

It was just a short crossing, on the ferry from Vatersay to Barra. In good weather, with the work done, folk would make the crossing just for an outing. There is a beautiful beach there and people would stroll the length of it and back. You walked on the white sand and looked one way to the high ground of Mingulay. Then you looked back to the stone tower of Kisimul's Castle. Some young lads were over and they were bantering away. But one of the lads noticed something a bit strange.

There was one woman they didn't know and she'd come over on the ferry too. She was standing on the beach and she was holding something behind her back. She was still standing in the same place, working away at the same thing, after all the boys had crossed the full length of the beach and come back. One lad was curious enough to stroll close. She had a long black tangle of kelp, holding each end up in the air.

When they were all boarding the ferry, to return, he noticed that the same woman had gone over to the other side of the boat and was still holding on to the black tangle.

'What has she got there?' he asked.

'Don't bother about her,' his mate said. 'She's a poor soul. She doesn't know that's no good to anyone.'

But there was something about the way she was holding on to it that made that lad know something was up. He sneaked over, taking out his pocket-knife. When she was looking the other way, he took his blade to the loop. He cut it in half.

A flood of thick milk came rushing out. You wouldn't have thought a volume like that could be contained in such a small space. It kept on gushing until it spilled over the side and on to the sea, white on the blue-green.

Somehow that woman had gotten all the cow's milk into that tangle. But she lost every drop of it again, that day.

Chrisella Ross, from Point in Lewis, translated a snatch of a song for me. She said it was from the village of Upper Bayble, on Lewis, and was probably composed in the nineteenth century. It's from an oral source and Chrisella didn't know of a written text. She told it to me like this:

> *It was the devil's work in the bag that spilled.*
> *There was crab claws.*
> *There were primroses.*
> *Long pieces of woven stuff*
> *To tie to the cow's tail.*
> *And then you could steal her milk.*
> *When you would put the cloak on your shoulder*
> *With everyone else asleep*

You'd walk the night like a Manx cat.
You wouldn't be stopped,
Jumping the little rivers.
And that would leave most of the cattle
Within a span of Tiumpan Head
Without milk, without contentment.
Mute, without their own voice.

References

The above telling is based on a recording of Nan MacPherson by Lisa Sinclair (see Bruford and MacDonald 88), and notes of my own conversation with Chrisella Ross, an Lanntair, Stornoway, November 2013.

Notes in Bruford and MacDonald give the source of a Tiree version of the tale. A very similar tradition was collected in the 1895–97 notebooks of Father Allan MacDonald, priest at Eriskay. Much of this material was published – often with condensations, misunderstandings and inaccuracies – in the writings of Ada Goodrich-Freer, gathered in *Outer Isles* (Constable, London, 1903).

Goodrich-Freer's travel writing has some interesting contemporary accounts, including references to the Flannan Isles lighthouse disaster and St Kilda. She mentions that the rents in the southern isles were sometimes paid to MacNeil by Manx shearwater but it is not clear that this refers to Mingulay. She also mentions the naturalist MacGillivray but refers to him as 'a native of Barra' when he was born in Aberdeen but raised in Harris.

For a faithful reproduction of the material collected by 'Father Allan' see Campbell and Hall, *Strange Things* (Routledge and Kegan Paul, London, 1968). Another story of a woman 'being possessed of mystic powers in the way of withdrawing the milk produce from her neighbour's cows to her own' is reproduced on p. 285. Apart from the question of ethics in the need to acknowledge sources properly, Father Allan's original notes are better storytelling.

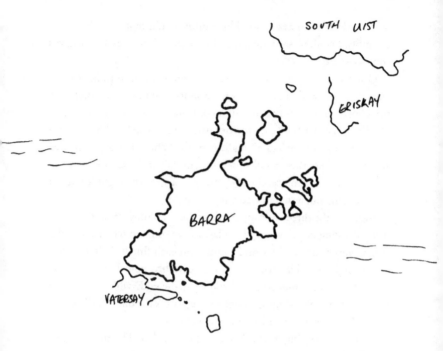

How the Down was Shared

The world was still very young. Not everything was settled. There were still a few things to work out. The seabirds were complaining that they didn't have enough down on them to keep warm through the winter. There was not going to be enough left to go round. All the seabirds gathered together. Every bird that could rise buoyant on a wave attended. Every bird that could strut along the shorelines was also there. You can imagine the shadows of all these wings, the combined noise of all these cries. It was a conference.

A fine old goose rose up on her broad feet, to speak first.

'All warmth comes from the sun,' she said. 'It's only the sun can decide for us.'

To make a very lengthy discussion short, that statement was agreed. They would need to go to the sun itself to pay their respects and ask for the stock of down to be shared out. But they could not all go.

So they decided to draw lots. Three birds would represent the whole assembly. I couldn't say why it was three exactly but it often is, when it comes to stories.

One from every species of seabird came forward to peck at twigs placed in the sand. Three twigs were shorter than all the others and these were caught in the bills of a cormorant, a duck and a seagull. Off they flew, without any further discussion or delay. The day was wearing on and they had a long way to fly. When they at last landed at a point where they could watch the sun fall and rise, they came to ground. But the sun was already getting ready for the night, tired out from sending out as much warmth as it could.

Together, the three said why they'd come, all piping up, in turn. The sun was trying not to yawn. 'I'm glad you've come to see me,' he said. 'You're very welcome here and I hope you each find a sheltered rock for the night. But I'll need to get to my own bed now. I have to bring another day in the morning. Tell you what,' he said, 'whichever of you rises first to thank me for the light I bring, that's the one who'll get the down. And it will go to all your descendents too.'

There was nothing much they could say to that. The sun dropped out of sight soon after. The three birds just stayed where they were, at the end of a headland. The cormorant and the seagull both decided they would stay up and keep watch. Neither of them trusted themselves to wake if they gave way to sleep. They were tired out after the long flight.

But the duck said nothing. She knew herself well enough to know she had no chance of remaining awake till sunrise. So she just put her head under her wing and nodded off. This was noticed.

The cormorant hissed to the seagull, 'Will you look at that one? After coming all this way. What chance does she have now?'

'Aye,' said the gull, 'We've the best plan, all right. Our long wait will be worth it.'

It was a struggle. Both the seagull and the cormorant managed to keep their eyes open, but only just. Finally the cormorant had to give in. Her long neck didn't help much. It was a struggle to hold that up. It sank to her wing. First, one eye closed and then the other. She was soon in a deep sleep. That left only the seagull still awake. No one to gossip to.

Day began to break at last. First the black sky went indigo. Then the first rosy fingers appeared in the east. The seagull couldn't hold herself back. You know what noisy birds they are anyway. Her squawking woke the duck.

'Look there,' the gull cried, 'himself is up at last.'

'Nearly,' said the duck. 'Thanks for waking me but you're a bit early. The sun's not over the sea yet.'

That was the duck wide awake now. She began to wash and preen herself so she was ready to welcome the sun. She looked around and noticed that the seagull had now fallen into deep sleep. The effort of crying out had taken her last strength. The seagull and the cormorant were now huddled with their heads on their wings.

The sky was soon all shades of red and yellow and orange. The duck called out, without thinking, just giving thanks for the day. She didn't have the prettiest call of the birds but it was a very happy sound.

The sun heard and saw it all. Right away, he granted that duck enough down for herself and for all her descendants, all they'd ever need.

Her contented quacks woke up the cormorant. The generous sun gave that bird enough to keep herself warm, even when diving deep. That too was shared out with his own descendants. At last the seagull woke. She was not left out. They'd all made an effort.

You see how the down was shared out in proportion to their early rising, from sunrise on. You might have noticed it's still like that. So that's why the duvet duck, I mean the eider duck, has the best share of all.

References

This is a type of story my own relations told me as a child. Our Arthur Mee's *The Children's Encyclopedia* was also a prolific source of world stories. This version is largely based on a version told on Barra by Rachel MacLeod. It was available on tape, with an accompanying book, under the title 'Am Bloigh Beag le Beannachd' and can be found in digital form at: http://www.ambaile.org.uk/en/item/item_audio. jsp?item_id=34592

The closest comparison I've found, thanks to Tom Muir, is one recorded in the Faroe Islands, transcribed, translated and published in *Chambers Journal*, 13 March 1886. In that version there are only two birds, the cormorant and the eider.

The story is also similar to aboriginal American traditions such as 'How the buzzard got its feathers', which has been recorded in many versions. Here is a link to one, which, like the Gaelic recording, is presented as a teaching resource: http://ils.unc.edu/~sturm/storytelling/ cuecards/buzzardfeathers.html.

DONALD AND THE SKULL

There was this fellow called Red Donald. That probably meant he had jet black hair, but anyway, he was out for a walk in the woods one day and came across something gleaming white, at the side of the path. He kicked the grasses and twigs aside to see what it was. The shine of the light on it made him curious. It turned out to be a human skull.

'What brought you here?' Donald said, bending to have a closer look.

'Too much speaking brought me here,' the skull replied. Donald nearly fell over with the shock of hearing that. He went, as fast as his legs could carry him, to the court of the king. He told the attendants he had something very remarkable to say and he could only tell it to the highest authority. The king didn't have much on that morning, and his own curiosity was aroused. Donald told him that he'd heard a skull speak and he could show his majesty's officers where it lay.

So he was given an escort of the kings' men and they all rode out to the point at the path where Donald remembered seeing the skull. Sure enough, they found it all right and they all hushed as Donald posed the question.

'What brought you here?'

Nothing was heard. He asked it again, and a third time, but still no sound was heard from the skull. 'You're in trouble now,' the head guard said. 'The king does not take kindly to time-wasters.'

The king himself heard the complaint. He thought he might at least get some entertainment out of Red Donald even if he did seem to be a liar. 'They tell me you asked your question three times and got no reply,' he said. 'You should lose your tongue for lying and the easiest way to do that is just to chop off your head and be done with it. But this court will give you a chance.'

Donald's face showed a glimmer of hope.

'I will now pose three questions to you. You have three days of freedom to consider your answers. Then you will be brought back here. If your answers are satisfactory, you will be released. And if they are not, you will lose your head.'

Red Donald was nervous now, but he certainly listened carefully.

'How long would it take me to go all the way round the world? Did you take that in?'

'Yes, your majesty, I did.'

'What exactly is the value of my entire property, my kingdom and everything in it, to the nearest coin?'

'Yes, I've taken that one in, too.'

'These will be a good warm-up for you. But you might have a bit more difficulty with my last question. And I'll tell you that one when you are brought back here.'

Red Donald did not enjoy his short-lived freedom very much. First, he was pacing the floor of his house without bothering to eat or drink. Then he was pacing the drive. Then who should come along but that scallywag of a Skyeman, Guilleasbuig Aotrom.

Some people said he was a fool and some people said he was wise. Whatever he was, he liked a challenge. 'You don't look too happy today, Red Donald. What's troubling you?'

When Guilleasbuig heard the sad tale he asked Donald if he could share the first two questions with him. He heard them and he nodded.

'But we have no way of knowing what the last one will be,' said Donald.

'No we don't,' said Gilleasbuig, 'but I think we might chance it all the same.'

He asked Donald to hand him his hat, jacket, breeks, shoes and everything, last thing on Thursday, so he could take his place for the appearance at the court first thing on Friday.

'But you'll lose your head if you fail.'

'I don't think I'm ready to let that go yet.'

Donald showed more anxiety than the man who was taking his place. The Skyeman liked to tackle authority in any shape or form. He seemed pretty confident.

No one realised that the fellow under the hat had a different face, certainly not the king, when he posed the first question.

'Can you answer me now, how long to go round the world?'

'That would take you twenty-four hours, precisely.'

'And how can you be so precise?'

'Because I'm assuming a king like yourself will want to go in time with the sun and that's how long the sun takes.'

The king admitted that was a good answer and moved on to the second question. 'And what am I worth?'

'You can't be worth more than twenty-nine pieces of silver.'

' You seem fairly certain of that too but I can assure you I'm worth a great deal more than that.'

'I beg to differ,' said Gilleasbuig. 'Our Lord was sold for thirty pieces and I don't think you can be worth more than that.'

Again the king could admit that was a good reply. He still had his ace to play.

'So are you ready for my third question.'

'I am.'

'What am I thinking?'

'You're thinking I'm Red Donald but I'm not. I'm Guilleasbuig Aotron,' he said, taking off Donald's hat.

Well, the king and everyone in earshot admitted they'd had very good entertainment, enough to make up for their wasted journey to see the miraculous skull. Donald had been fidgeting and fretting, not very far away. He was very glad to see the man who'd taken his place walk out of there. They took a stroll through the woods again, taking the same path home.

What should they see but the bleached white skull again. Donald gave it a kick. 'What brought you here anyway, getting me into trouble like that?'

'Too much speaking brought me here,' said the skull.

References
Donald John MacKinnon, Barra, recorded by Peter Cooke and Morag MacLeod, in Bruford and MacDonald 30c. This is one of three Scottish versions of a tale with three questions in that collection.

Similar questions and riddles are linked to stories of the now mythic historical character George Buchanan. One recording, held in the School of Scottish Studies, has the question 'How many ladders to reach the moon?' rather than 'What am I worth?' I've adapted this tradition, imported into my own version of *The Blue Men of the Stream*, as it seems to me there are endless variations of the questions and they do seem to pass from story to story.

The tradition of addressing a skull as a symbol of mortality is, of course, common, though this story takes a playful approach. Old gravestones at the Eye cemetery, Aignish Lewis, have excellent examples of a warning engraved, as do carvings at St Clement's church, Rodel. Chrisella Ross also quotes religious verse from the Point district of Lewis which has a conversation with a skull at its heart. From one Dugald Buchanan, an evangelical, writing in the late eighteenth century in *An Claigeann*, Chrisella suggested the tone is also playful and satiric, 'stark and dark armies of maggots marching in and out of the skull' (personal conversation).

Notes in Bruford and MacDonald link this with a tale told in different parts of Africa and also one appearing in African-American culture. As it happens, I heard the phrasing of the lines which frame the story, 'Too much speaking brought me here', from Liam Crause. He is a Gaelic speaker from Rhode Island, USA, a musician and singer and student of Gaelic culture (Bruford and MacDonald quote the slightly different phrasing, 'Speaking brought me here'). There is a suggestion that the tale could have been passed to Barra by crew members of visiting ships. As a former coastguard officer who worked with many ex-Merchant Navy seamen, I'd suggest that the tradition of sailors returning from their travels with new stories, or new versions of old stories, continues to this day. This is distinct from tales of incidents which occurred during voyages. There are two strong examples of that line of storytelling in the tales from Angus MacLellan, collected and translated by John Lorne Campbell, *Stories from South Uist* (still available from Birlinn). The retired Western Isles harbour-master, Roddy Jardine, told me a very fine seaman's yarn in November 2013, proving that this source of new tales continues.

The Cask in the Foc'sle

When I grew up in Stornoway in the 1950s and '60s, a sailing vessel of any kind was a very rare sight. All the kids I knew haunted the piers. We all envied those who would be taken out in small boats to catch the plentiful haddock and whiting and many other species which could be found without going even as far as Arnish lighthouse. One Saturday I was dangling a line off Number One pier as usual when I recognised the boys in a large open boat with a sailing rig. They were mates of my big brother and their father was taking them sailing. For a minute it looked like I'd be asked to come down the ladder and join them. But the boat was pushed out and the gap widened fast. The father and skipper probably reckoned he couldn't take me aboard without asking my parents first.

He did me a great favour because from then on I was even more determined to get sailing. It's gone together with hearing and telling stories ever since.

In 2013, I met one of the lads who was in that craft. Roddy Jardine had just retired from his position as Western Isles Harbour Master and I found that he was living in Castlebay rather than Stornoway. At the invitation of Ruth Brennan and Stephen Hurrel, a social-scientist and an artist, I was there to join their collaborative art-science project Sgeulachdan na Mara/ Sea Stories: Barra, *an online cultural map of the sea. That weekend proved to me conclusively that telling tales linked to named points or islands or reefs is not only a thing of the past. But Roddy leaned over and told me, with breathtaking fluency, an example of the story a merchant seaman brought back home, on leave from his ship. This is not an accurate transcription. I'm thinking back to the conversation at the impressive Heritage and Cultural Centre in Castlebay and trying to pass the gist of it on. But I have checked it over with Roddy since then.*

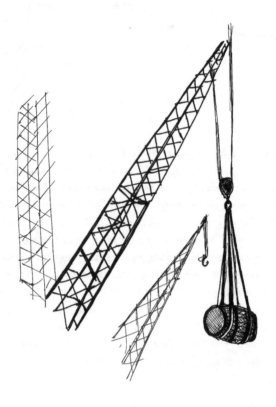

We were in dock in Antwerp, loading a cargo bound for Mexico. Ships were by no means dry in these days. You just didn't think of it if you were going on watch. But, when you knocked off, you could take a beer or a dram. And that was that. We'd done not bad for runs ashore but the cargo was just about all stowed. We only had to take our own stores aboard. These had arrived, from Glasgow, and were all ready and waiting for us.

The company has just adopted a new system for ships' stores. Everything was checked in Glasgow and sealed. As long as the seals were intact, we could accept them at our port of departure, without having to account for every tin of Brasso. Soon they were being hoisted in our own derricks and we were about ready for the off. The tugs were getting into gear. But there was a holdup.

There were twenty-five unmarked boxes and a wooden barrel. The warehouseman insisted they were ours and they weren't getting left behind. There was no barrel of anything on our own list. It was a Saturday and this man was going to a football match. Our pilot was aboard. It was easier to take the lot rather than risk a big scene and delay our sailing.

Once we were clear of the locks and the tugs were slipped, a curious group formed around the barrel. The bung was eased out, with a marlin spike. The mate was a sober sort and reckoned it was paraffin in an old wine barrel. The Spanish bosun said it was brandy. The second mate was from Skye but he said nothing at all. He sent the cadet for a dipper so a proper sample could be drawn through the bunghole.

It could have been anything at all but after a wary sip he took a good mouthful and grinned from ear to ear. We had taken on board 40 gallons or 5,920 quarter-gill measures of quality whisky. This needed a proper consultation of all the officers. The captain was old school and fairly authoritarian but he decreed that, as long as the privilege was not abused, the barrel could be housed in the foc'sle till our return to Antwerp. Any slight loss of contents could be put down to evaporation in the tropics.

Amongst the general cargo, there happened to be a quantity of glass decanters, bound for the World Cup, which you might remember was in Mexico that year. There were bound to be some breakages along the way, so this was avoided, for some, by being liberated and shared between the cabins. The hose from the ship's washing machine was borrowed, from time to time, to make checks on the state of the liquid in our charge.

The return voyage passed without incident and all too soon we were again tied up in Antwerp. No one asked about the barrel. We were in Le Havre when the customs inspectors came aboard. At that time the 'top shelf' magazines were a bit of an issue and the inspectors found a few in the crew's quarters. They thought it might be a good idea to make a thorough search for any more hidden literature. As the junior mate, I was given a big bunch of keys and asked to show them every corner of the ship. Once we were in the fo'csle, one of them strolled over to the cask, propped there on its stand, bung side up. 'What's in that?' he asked, in plain English. I answered him truthfully, in plain English. 'That barrel is nearly full of the best malt whisky.'

He began to laugh. He then shouted over to his colleagues, in French, and they also all started to laugh. It's possible they did not believe me. So they turned away from our cask of single malt and carried on searching for the erotica which was not aboard.

When we set sail again, our cask was still with us, though it might have been a little lighter. We hit some heavy weather close to the Azores. There was no doubt about it. The ship was down at the head. We had to rig deck-lines to go forward. Sea-water was being trapped between decks up front. We had to get into the foc'sle to free off the drainage holes that would allow it to run off. Water is heavy stuff. The pumps could not reach that.

We couldn't get the bulkhead door open. There was a banging and thumping. I looked at the bosun and he looked at me. Our cask must have floated free and was now wedged against the door we were trying to open in order to save the ship. We could ease it back a few inches, but not enough to let anyone in. The mate went for a fire-axe. It was already swinging when the second mate pleaded for one more attempt with a crowbar.

It must have been his determination, but he saved both the barrel and the ship. After that, the remaining contents were decanted into this and that container and shared between us all. The barrel was broken up and the ship continued on her route.

References

The research by Ruth Brennan and Stephen Hurrel proves that stories linked to place are still widely told, as premonitions and inexplicable incidents. Many of the recent traditions they have recorded and presented are like a contemporary version of the traditions collected by Father Allan. *The Sea Stories* cultural map of the sea was part of the Cape Farewell Sea Change exhibition at the Royal Botanic Gardens Edinburgh (2013–14). This project exhibited the collaborative and independent work of artists and scientists, considering the relationships between people, place and resources.

To me, vernacular tales, whether traditional or contemporary, often carry a sense that our very survival is on a knife-edge. A degree or two difference in sea temperature or the height of tide can change everything.

But a yarn like Roddy's is also typical. Hebridean stories are not all doom and gloom. It is important in showing how the tales of the returning traveller still feed into the stock of island stories. I have also heard a more historical but equally good-natured tale from Roddy's brother, David Jardine, but that one is linked to Stornoway so we'll come to it further up the map.

THE POINT WHERE ENGLISH WAS SPOKEN

Moving northwards from the main harbour at Castlebay, on Barra, you come to another inlet of sea. This one is called Brevig Bay. From the shore, you're looking out from there to the Sea of the Hebrides. The headland which reaches out to that sea, on the north side of the bay, is a good vantage point. That's where the coastguard hut was built.

The first version was fixed in place there in the 1940s. Two or three neighbours used to do shifts. They would keep watch if bad weather was expected. That first hut was made of wood. There was hardly space to turn a chair. The girls from the village would be sent down there carrying a big pot of tea. It would be an earthenware pot, wrapped in a towel.

When a woman from the next croft would milk her cow, down at the point, she would put aside a jug of fresh milk for the men who took their turn in the Lookout. They were very glad of that and the crofters and their children were only too happy to help. They might also get a story or two.

The men did long watches, then. Later on, they had a paraffin stove of their own and later still, the wooden hut was replaced with one made from solid blocks.

All of the village children loved going down to the hut. Sometimes there would be a real crowd in there. The evening would pass, with stories washed down with tea. Of course there was a telephone installed by that time. Then there was a radio. The sounds that came over the coastguard radio were strange to the ears of the younger children from the surrounding area. Communications were in a language foreign to them until they went to school – English.

But way back, even before the croft at Leinish was divided, there was a woman from the generation gone before used to do her milking out at that point. She always said she could hear voices. There was no hut there then and no one knew of any plans to put one there. But she would hear voices. There wasn't a soul to be seen but she was hearing people speaking, all right. And there was something else. The voices were speaking in a language she couldn't understand.

Because she couldn't make out what they were saying, she thought they might be speaking in English. The story spread round until the point was known, years and years back, as Creag nam Beurla – the point where English was spoken.

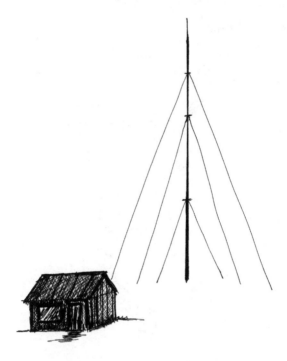

Remember now, that point was known by that name about forty years before the coastguard hut was put up and the telephone or the radio was installed.

References
Retold from a recording of Katie Douglas, Leinish, Barra, collected by Eoin MacNeil (Voluntary Action Barra and Vatersay) as part of the project *Sgeulachdan na Mara* Sea Stories: Barra. Recordings of local stories and lore made in 2012 and 2013 can be accessed online, in an interactive cultural map of the sea. The research carried out by this team, a social scientist and an artist, in collaboration with the local community (who will continue to collect and add new sea stories over the years to come) shows the continuing interest in stories ranging from inexplicable happenings to the lore behind the local names for points or reefs. See http://www.mappingthesea.net and http://www. capefarewell.com/seachange/barra-maps/

WORDS OF HELP

A man, by the name of Angus, sadly lost his wife. He was left to raise their one child. He did marry again and his new wife was very good to the child she was now responsible for.

All went well till one day the child's shirt could not be found anywhere in the house. Angus blamed his wife for this, saying she should be more careful. He said the loss showed that she did not truly care for the child as if it was her own.

Naturally she was hurt by these hard words, said in anger. But her husband did not take them back. Instead he'd lose no chance to say how she was neglecting his firstborn. In due course they were due to have their own child together. The birth went well but the mother was, of course, exhausted.

A healing hot drink was left at her bedside. But when she reached out for it she found the cup overturned and the liquid spilled. This happened not once but twice. The third time, the fresh hot drink was brought to her bedside and she was able to sip its goodness.

She made a full recovery and both children thrived. But one day, when the husband was working down the croft, taking the first child along with him, the dead mother of the firstborn paid a visit to the new wife. She was alone in the house, except for the baby in the cradle. The pale figure said not to be afraid. She wished no harm to either mother or child. She had to make this visit because she needed to thank her for fully taking on the duty of care passed on.

'You've looked after him as if he was your own,' she said. 'I couldn't rest, hearing the things that man's been saying to you. And I couldn't keep away when I saw you were in danger. It was the warm drink after childbirth which brought the infection I died from,' she said. 'The peats were smoking but not blazing and the water was never boiled. The smoke and dust went into it but it was never heated through. That's why I had to spill your own drink twice till I saw there was a good flame under the pot, the third time.'

The visitor had one more thing to say. 'And the bairn's shirt. I'll tell you where you'll find that. It was Angus's own hand that lost it, by accident. It was plucked up in the dark along with a bundle of straw. He used that to stop a draft in the byre. You should ask him to look again at the crack he stopped-up and he'll see how it was lost.'

That was all she needed to say. She could go back to her rest.

When the second wife steered her husband to the bairn's lost shirt, he saw that he'd been unjust. From then on, everyone in that family looked after each other.

References

From the notebooks of Father Allan MacDonald quoted in John L. Campbell and Trevor H. Hall, *Strange Things* (Routledge and Kegan Paul, London, 1968, no. 20, p. 286), recorded from Duncan MacInnes quoting Mrs Donald MacInnes, from Barra, living then in Eriskay.

The notebooks are an invaluable resource, the result of a sensitive man, committed to the culture and language of the people he lived amongst. Most scholars, including Alexander Carmichael (compiler of *Carmina Gadelica*) felt that his generosity with the material was abused when he shared it with the 'psychic researcher' Ada Goodrich-Freer, who published a large body of it without fully acknowledging that the collecting and collating, from the original Gaelic, was all done by Father MacDonald. *Strange Things* contains a very full summary of the issues as well as an invaluable group of English-language versions of traditions and tales, practical, supernatural and religious, from the southern islands of the Outer Hebrides.

Compare with no. 54 Bruford and MacDonald, *The Pabbay Mother's Ghost*, from Nan MacKinnon.

2

SOUTH UIST

The Crop-Headed Freckled Lass

There's been more than one laird thought himself a wise man. One such laird had before him a tenant accused of poaching a deer. A man at the far end of the village bore a grudge against this fellow and pointed out the place where the guts and head were buried. There was no arguing with that. In a sporting way, the laird said that he would give his tenant a chance to avoid eviction. He would pose three questions and grant him three days only, to consider them. He would hear his answers when they next met and that would decide his fate.

These were the questions:

'What is the richest thing in the world? No matter how much you take, it will be no worse off?'

The second was, 'What is the most poor?'

And the third, 'What creature goes first on four feet, then on two and finally goes on three?'

The poor man went home as if he was a condemned man. His eyes were on the ground and even his wife could not get him to speak. Luckily they were blessed with an unusual daughter. Some said she was not much to look at – she liked to wear her hair cropped short, like a lad's, and she was freckled. But she had a head on her shoulders all right. She was also a caring sort and her mother sent her to have a word with her father.

He told her they only had three days in the house. The roof would be burned and they'd be cast out unless he could answer three impossible questions. Soon she'd teased the three questions out of him.

'Well, father,' she said, 'I think you should come through and take your soup. We can sort this out, between us, all right.'

So they took their food and had a talk and the father of the crop-haired freckled lass began to cheer up. By the day of his appointment with the laird, he was quite confident.

'So what will never be any poorer, no matter what you take from it?' asked the laird.

'That would be the ocean itself. Take what you want, the rains will fall and it will be filled to its own level again.'

The laird admitted that was a suitable answer. 'And the poorest thing?'

'That would be fire. It consumes all so there's nothing but ashes left. You could feed it with all the richest things in the world and it would be no better off.'

'I don't think you thought of that one yourself,' the laird said. 'And the third question?' he asked. 'Do you remember that one?'

'Aye and the answer to it. My own daughter reminded me when she was young she could only move herself on hands and feet. So that would be like four legs. But once she was able to get up on the two legs, that was that. And yet she's seen an old man like your own father reach for a stick to help him walk. So that would be the three legs.'

The other man didn't know whether to be angry or impressed. 'I wouldn't mind meeting this daughter of yours,' he said.

'I think we could arrange that,' the free man said.

It was obvious the laird was fascinated as well as surprised at the wit in this free-thinking girl, who seemed to have her own way of doing things, even down to wearing her hair cropped like a boy's. She matched him, point by point, in the exchange. He visited more than once. Eventually he cried out, 'Well, if you were yourself the daughter of a laird, I would need to ask for your hand.'

'And if you were to decide to marry a lady, would you grant her something from your estate?'

'Naturally.'

'Well, I've no use now for anything you can give me but would you grant my father title to his house and bit of ground?'

'That's not a huge thing to ask. I think we could do that, since you replied so well to the three questions.'

She took him at his word and had him sign there and then to an agreement to hand over title of house and croft to her father.

'So now that my father is a laird, I must be the daughter of one,' she said.

He was taken by surprise and proposed on the spot.

'No, I won't marry you,' said the crop-haired, freckled daughter. 'You asked me on a whim and you could change your mind on a whim. You could throw me out without a thing. I'd need some security.'

'What would you need?'

'You asked my father to answer three questions so I would make a similar condition.'

'And what would that be?'

'That you sign an agreement. In the event of demanding that I leave your house, I might take three things of my choice with me.'

The laird was now so taken by the flashing eyes and quick mind in that boyish head that he agreed to her condition. Everything was done properly. They had a fine wedding and she moved to the big house. Before long they were blessed with an heir. He had done all right for himself because she was a good mother and ran the estate better than any manager. People knew they could trust her and in turn they did not want to deceive one of their own.

All went well till there was a dispute between two tenants. One had a mare in foal and one had a strong gelding. At that time, animals would be put out together on the common grazings. At the end of the summer the mare had foaled and the foal had grown. It would run with the gelding most of the day. When the animals returned to the crofts in autumn, the foal kept close to the gelding. Of course the owner asked for her back and the other fellow said that the animal had made its own choice.

They put it to the laird, to save going to law. He had them take the two horses and the foal to the middle of a field. There was a gate in the dyke to the north and another to the south. Each of the crofters walked to a different gate, one with the mare and the other leading the gelding. The foal followed the gelding through the south gate and the laird said that was it decided.

But the owner of the mare came to see the crop-haired, freckled girl, now the wife of the laird. 'I'll tell you what to do,' she said, 'but you must never let the laird know it was me who gave you the idea.' He agreed to that.

Next day the owner of the mare went out, taking some salt in a sack. He walked down to the loch where he could see the laird was casting a fly. He walked up and down, close by, sowing the salt in the damp hollows, within sight of the laird.

Sure enough he came up, out of curiosity and saw what he saw. 'What on earth are you up to?'

His tenant told him he was sowing the salt in the damp places to be sure of getting a good return of a valuable commodity.

'Don't be a fool, man. You know perfectly well that the salt will dissolve rather than grow.'

'Well sir, I think it's just as likely that salt will grow as a gelding produce a fine foal.'

'You didn't think of that one on your own,' the laird said. And he didn't give up till the poor man admitted it was his own wife who had advised him what to say.

The laird went home in a rage. 'I can't have you interfering with the business of the estate, making me look a fool. You'll leave this house right now,' he said.

'Fine,' she said, 'but I'm allowed three things to carry with me.'

'Take them and go.'

The crop-headed, freckled wife lifted up the cradle, complete with their son and heir, and carried it back over the threshold. Then she returned and carried out the small locked chest which she knew contained the title deeds to the entire estate.

The laird sat on a chair in amazement. But she came back in and carried that out with him still sitting in it. She left him outside and went back in herself. First she carried in the cradle with the heir. And then she carried the chest with the title deeds, back in to her house.

She called out to the baffled man, still seated in his chair, out on the grass. 'Away with you now,' she said. 'You were going to evict my father and all of us but we're the lairds now. Best be on your way.' She turned the key in the door.

He pleaded with her and promised she could run things her own way if she let him back in. At last she relented and he did keep his word, well aware of the value of the crop-headed, freckled woman who was now his wife.

References
Based on several versions but often linked to South Uist, as told by Angus MacLellan, 'The Three Questions and the Three Burdens', in *Stories from South Uist*, translated by John Lorne Campbell (Routledge and Kegan Paul, London, 1961, now republished by Birlinn, Edinburgh, p. 70). Source traced to Skye and classed as Arne Thompson, no. 875, *The Clever Peasant Girl*. John Lorne Campbell notes Irish examples and another related to poaching, from Duncan MacDonald from Penerine, recorded at Lochboisdale, 1950.

Compare that with the lively storytelling of Peter Stewart, a traveller settled in Barvas, Isle of Lewis, in 'The Poor Man's Clever Daughter' (Bruford and MacDonald, no. 32). This is an excellent example of how timeless and placeless stories survived amongst travelling folk, to be shared with the communities they visited or settled in. Another example of this is the strange tale of the woman who ran with the deer but returned when her husband was to be remarried. For me this invites comparison with versions of the Selkie legend, but also with the Gotland tale of the sea nymph in which a man vanishes for many years and reappears from an underwater kingdom on the day his wife is remarried.

In 1901 Carmichael visited Barra. He describes meeting the itinerant tinsmith Alexander MacDonald and his wife Isabella. They were living in a homemade tent and would not accept any payment for their time. Isabella sang a ballad which contains the story: see Alexander Carmichael, *Carmina Gadelica* (Scottish Academic Press, 1971, p. 338)

The Kingfish

You might have got the idea by now that fish matter quite a lot to us in the Outer Hebrides. People will talk for hours about whether haddock or whiting make the better eating. Most islanders prefer ling to cod, but lythe or pollack are favoured in some parts and not in others. So the lythe is sometimes known as iasg baintighearna *or 'lady's fish', probably due to its delicate flesh.* Along some of our coasts they consider the spurdog or biorach a curse, and in others it's a staple food and so a species sought with long-lines.*

Another Lewisman describes the latter species well:

> *The general outline of the body is cylindrical and is of brownish grey, slightly tinted with a dusky red and the belly is white and the skin tough like sandpaper. There are two dorsal fins, each of which is armed on the anterior edge with a sharp and slightly curved spine. In order to strike with these instruments the fish first bends itself into a bow and with a jerking motion the body rebounds in the opposite direction and in this manner the creature seldom misses the object aimed at.* **

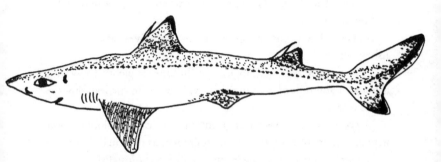

The friend I've never met, Morrison the cooper (whose volumes in manuscript are held at the library a couple of hundred yards from my door), noted how a laird of the Clanranald family, in South Uist, much preferred the kingfish or spotted dogfish to the spurdog. He employed one Angus Roy to do nothing much else but fish for that species, to put on his table. Clanranald did not turn his nose up at the occasional sole or brill or turbot, though of course he was too proud to be seen turning the flatfish over or picking out the backbone when he'd eaten the top fillet from the bone. One time he was heard to wish there was another such fish to follow the first. It was, of course, Angus Roy who had the nerve to ask his chief to turn his head for a moment. Then he took hold of a matching dinner plate, put it on top of the other and with one deft movement reversed their positions so there appeared to be an intact flatfish on the new one, pale side up.

But in some seasons, the lesser spotted dogfish, the one he considered a more tender fish at the table, was in short supply. Angus Roy would then set a line over the banks where the larger species, the spurdog, were running. He took the precaution of snipping the spines from them, in case his catch should be sighted before he had peeled the firm fillets from the rasping skin.

Sure enough, one day the laird himself was talking a stroll by the pier and saw his fisherman's catch before it was skinned.

'My word,' said the laird, feeling no spine at the dorsals, 'these are very large for kingfish and very scarcely spotted.'

'They are indeed,' said Angus Roy. 'The survivors of summer and autumn and the first part of the winter grow to a good size, if you can find them. And the speckles only appear when they've been dead for an hour or two.'

'And how do you find this species at this time of year when no other fisherman can?'

'I sow the grounds,' said Angus Roy. 'In times of plenty, I sow with the spawn and milt of the full fishes, with an eye to the lean months of the year.'

Maybe Clanranald wasn't as green as he was cabbage-looking and kept Angus on as much for the entertainment as the catch. But there is, of course, a reason why the spotted dogfish is the kingfish.

Back in the days when the Hebrides were more Norse than Scots, the king of Lochlinn (Norway) and the king of Scotland met in South Uist. No doubt they had business to discuss but that didn't stop them taking a boat out and casting out their handlines. The king of Scotland had a pull but knew to bide a moment till the fish that was nudging his bait took it properly. He was delighted to see it was the *dallag* or spotted dogfish. But he was not so happy to see that there was another hook and line in it, once he'd pulled it aboard.

By that time the king of Lochlinn had woken up to the jerks on his own line and claimed the fish for himself. The Norwegian's hook was deeper down than the iron cast by the Scottish king.

'Aye,' said the Scot, 'But you felt nothing. It was my own skill brought that fish to the boat.'

An argument started that went on for days. Each put his point and counter-point until at last there was nothing left but to take the matter to law. The dogfish must have been well brined or dried or both by the time a finding was made. The court found in favour of the Scottish king as he had first sensed the fish.

It was a wonder the incident did not lead to war, but it did lead to a special value being placed on the fish that two kings thought worth arguing over. From that day, in the Hebrides, the spotted dogfish was known as the kingfish.

References
* See the Carmichael Watson collection, Edinburgh University: http://www.carmichaelwatson.lib.ed.ac.uk/cwatson/en
** *My Story*, Norman Morrison, Inverness, 1937.
The kingfish story is in vol. 1 of J.L. Campbell, collected from *South Uist*.

Two Ravens

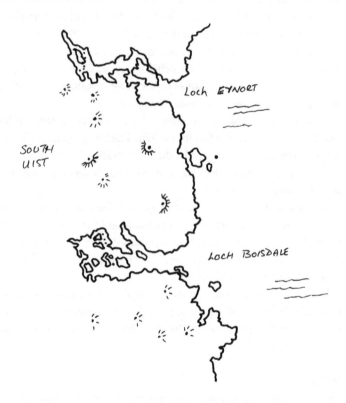

Alasdair of Lochboisdale was known far and wide as a skilful and canny farmer. His herds grew but the beasts were known as much for their quality as their number. He could sell them for breeding as well as for meat. He was also a strong fellow and would walk the hills for miles. Many a local woman cast a glance in his direction but they all knew he was destined to make a match with a higher circle of Highland society.

It was no real surprise when his family met with the MacLeods of Dunvegan who, at that time, had an unmarried daughter known for her looks and her wit. That family had perhaps lost some of their wealth, but they did have their name and their castle. And the family of Alasdair of the Cattle now had stock and wealth and a good name in the trade. So there were no real obstacles and the arrangements were made to hold a *reitach*. That's the engagement ceremony which concludes such an arrangement and, I'm told, required as much whisky as the wedding itself.

Alasdair was to cross to it by his own vessel, of course. The family had more than one seaworthy birlinn, well capable of crossing the Little Minch. They set out in fair weather but, as soon as they had Dunvegan Head in sight, things began to go wrong. On a sailing vessel, it's often not one thing but a line of events – none of them a great problem in itself, but they build towards a disaster. A sheet-rope or halyard could snap or a sail could be ripped or an oar lost. These are often short-lived difficulties but sometimes they accumulate so you lose control at a vital moment. All along that coast, violent squalls are known to thrust down from the high ground to the sea. It's no place to lose way on a vessel.

Alasdair was anxious and could see the run of bad luck leading them into serious difficulty. He looked all about for signs of the cause of their troubles. High over the mast he saw two ravens, keeping time in the air with the slow progress of their craft. It was common to see gannets or fulmar or kittiwakes or shearwater or petrel or great skua but far less common to see ravens at sea. Something in the flight of these birds raised Alasdair's suspicions. He primed his gun and put it to his shoulder.

There was a flurry of black feathers from one of the birds. It did not fall but, at that, the two of them fell back from the air above the boat and soon disappeared from sight.

Repairs were made and the vessel reached the safety of Loch Dunvegan. She was put on a safe anchorage and the party was made welcome in preparation for the *reitach*.

But Alasdair of Boisdale sensed that something was the matter in the castle. One of his lads spoke with a serving girl and discovered the story. It seems that some of the MacLeods were not so sure about this match, whatever head of beasts the Lochboisdale clan could claim. Some of the Dunvegan family put more store on title than on stock. Two ladies of the castle, maidservants to the daughter promised to Alasdair, were known to have argued against the match.

But the Uist family had arrived and the ceremony was to be done. The Lochboisdale people were introduced to the MacLeods of Dunvegan as soon as they had taken some rest and washed the salt from their faces.

The two maidservants of the highest rank were indeed present at the gathering. But one of them had just suffered an accident. Her right arm was bandaged up in a sling.

Alasdair knew then that they had done their worst to prevent the match. After the business of the day was done, drams were taken and goodwill prevailed. He took the opportunity to speak to the two maidservants, calling them aside from the gathering which was now growing very lively. The pipers were having their time. 'Now don't be afraid of me,' he said. 'I bear you no grudge as long as you now accept what's been decided here.'

He called for his gun and again told them that neither had anything to fear. 'There have been too many from Skye and from the Uists lost in feuding and disputes,' he said.

He put the tip of his gun to the wound which he knew to be in that woman's injured shoulder. He turned it three times sunwise around the damaged area. They say she made a very swift recovery and never again argued against the coming together of the families.

References

I heard this from Chrisella Ross in an Lanntair, Stornoway, November 2013. My retelling is based on memory and some handwritten notes. She ascribed the original source to one Lachlan Mor (mac Dhomhnaill 'ic Mhuirich), one of the dynasty of MacVurichs, bards to Clanranald. Chrisella said that a recording of the story was indeed in the School of Scottish Studies archive. I felt I should tell it first, remembering the essence of her own account, to catch the spirit of the ongoing spoken tale, before researching further.

The role of Clanranald features strongly in the learned, illustrated travelogue of Professor Murdo MacDonald. This resource is a generous sharing of the author's personal recollections. These are brimful of cultural references, ranging from the culture of seafaring to a summary of the marks that artist-makers have left in the landscape of the Highlands and Islands over centuries: www.murdomacdonald.wordpress.com.

THE COOPER'S BEAUTIFUL DAUGHTER

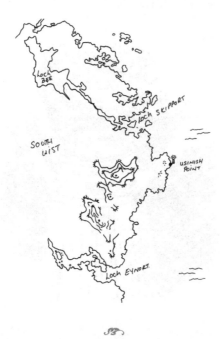

In the days of prosperity, when the herring were thick in all the seas surrounding the Outer Hebrides, the quays of our harbours were stacked
with barrels. The Baltic Traders would ghost in to Loch Eynort, Loch
Skiport and Lochmaddy to load the precious cargo. It was not only
the merchants and fishers who did well. The coopers' trade was a good
skill to have, in those days.

One master cooper happened to have a daughter of exceptional
beauty. She was sharp-witted but not sharp in nature so there was no
shortage of admirers. Three of those became regular visitors. I think
the man of the house was getting a bit fed up of the clutter about the
place so he asked his daughter to make sure the three main contenders
visited on the same night.

The lads found a part-made barrel waiting for them. There was a
hammer and the hoops which hold the staves together. 'Let's see you
show your skills, lads.'

Of course none of the three had ever taken a close look at a barrel in
their lives, though it was a thing you used every day.

But the daughter whispered a word in the ear of one of the three,
'Be sure and be the last to try.'

The braw lad who went first was eager to show his strength. He gave the hoop a couple of severe clouts with the hammer and it went so far down the bulge of the barrel that it parted. That was him out of the game.

The second thought he'd learn from the first but was that bit too timid, so the hoop didn't go far enough to get a grip.

It was time for another whisper. 'When the hoop stops going down, my father stops driving it.'

This fellow had a positive touch with the hammer but watched the progress of the hoop and judged when it was a good fit.

'That's the one for you,' the father said and, strangely enough, the daughter agreed.

References

This is another story which has gone across the pond. In my own retelling I've returned it in Uist, in the same way as the film producer Bill MacLeod reset the Alastair MacLeod short story 'The Lost Salt Gift of Blood' in the Isle of Harris for his BBC production. The source of this tale is another excellent collection of traditional material from a gifted performer, recorded, edited and translated by John Shaw: *Brìgh an Òrain – A Story In Every Song: the Songs and Tales of Lauchie MacLellan* (McGill-Queen's University Press, Quebec, 2000).

ASKING FOR THE WIND

There was the storyteller and there was the bard. Some would say that the storyteller could take you through the range of human emotions while the bard could recite fluent and eloquent language to celebrate the family who was supporting him. But I don't think it could ever have been as simple as that. There are bards who wrote satire and those who celebrated ordinary people who could never pay the one who composed the verse. And there are storytellers who could make the language ring as fluently as any rhythmic verse.

But then there were the MacVurichs. People say that the output of this family of bards, who composed across the centuries, amounted to cartloads of manuscripts, but that all of it was of high quality. You can judge for yourselves because much of it has been kept safe. Some people say that poetry is powerful and others say that it changes nothing. There are many traditions to say that at least one MacVurich had astonishing powers. The family lived at Staligarry in South Uist and wrote many lines to commemorate the doings of the Clanranald chiefs. But when times were lean in the bardic business, MacVurich would use his skills in navigation to ferry people back and fore from Skye. And they also said that his famous eloquence could have strange powers.

MacVurich had put in to Canna. They met a merchant who was keen to return to Arisaig, over on the mainland. MacVurich's son was also aboard and was very keen to get home. Maybe this lad was court-ing, back on the Uists. What do you do, as a skipper, when everyone aboard wants to go to a different place? And most skippers are content to get a mild, fair wind, without too much drama, though they'll deal with a gale if they meet it.

The skipper said that each should raise his voice to request the wind that would suit his purpose. But he used his rank and put in a very fair request for the warm south-westerly, which would put the wind a little behind their beam as they made to clear Usinish Point and tuck in to the safety of Loch Skiport. There's an anchorage in there, called the Wizard's Pool, where no wind will bother a vessel. This was his formula:

> A south wind from calm Gailbhinn,
> as the King of Elements ordained;
> one we could ride without rowing or tacking
> a breeze that could bring us no harm.

MacVurich quoted from a goatherd of the King of Norway who felt he was in a warm, fertile and temperate land when he set foot on 'Gailbhinn', which could well be Galway. So that would be a temper-ate south-westerly breeze, taken mid-ships or, as he would have said, *ga ruith air a tarsainn*. Now they could cross where he wanted, on one tack.

'What kind of a soft skipper have we got here?' said the merchant. 'She could take a wind with a bit more body in it. And one that could take me at once to my next port of call.'

'Well you can ask for it yourself,' MacVurich said. Not for the first time, one action, not fatal in itself to safe navigation, set off a chain of events. This was the merchant's plea:

A North wind, hard as a rod of iron
to raise her gunwales high on the crests,
so she has the strength and speed of a hind
running down the hard peak of a hill.

Before long, there was indeed a backing of the wind, to the tune of 180 degrees. The building waves threw her bow off their course and they had no option but to run before it, taking it on their port quarter. This was a fast and exhilarating point of sail, a broad reach to take her, nearly surfing, as her rounded, buoyant stern lifted on the following seas (*Ga ruith air a sliasaid*). It looked like they might be bound for Arisaig after all. But there was one request still to be said. Mind you, they also say you should never make use of that third one. It's a bit like unleashing the last knot.

MacVurich, the skipper, had referred to the land favoured by the King's goatherd, the one who became a smith like no other. That was a man who could temper the sword of Finn to endow it with power. But now the skipper's son wanted home and did his best to raise the wind that would turn them round again. The lad referred to one of the strongest of the Fingallian warriors. Even Finn was relieved when Conan placed his spear with the Fianna rather than against them. Now the son of MacVurich looked to wake his spirit:

If in cold hell there's a wind
that turns the waves' sides to red,
Conan, send it after me
in fiery flaming sparks.

It wouldn't matter, he said, if the power of it was such that only his father, himself and their black dog could take it.

That's what they got, all right. The boat was whipped round, beyond the control of anyone aboard it. It was driven by the squalls that came from clouds like anvils, looming from the heights above the jagged line of the Cuilins of Rum. There was hail and there was lightning. They had to let go the halyard and pull all cloth down. Now they were running (*ga ruith air a deireadh*) where the wind and waves drove them, pushed by the gale on the bare pole. She was driven into a place, close to Usinish Point. She came ashore with a crack that broke her in two. They were lucky to escape with their lives and even the dog had a struggle in reaching dry land. All of them were beyond caring what land they stood on, as long as it was solid ground.

'What a chasm you took us into,' MacVurich's son said, though it was his own verse that had done the damage.

'Well I don't think we'll try that again,' his father said. 'From now on, we'll just put up with the wind we get.'

But to this day, the place where they made their landfall is still called A Ghiamraidh or 'The Chasm'.

References

This telling uses elements from several versions including recordings of Angus MacLellan and two from Martin MacIntryre, of Skye, made by D.A. MacDonald. Angus MacLellan's telling of this story is in *Stories From South Uist*, edited and translated by John Lorne Campbell. There is also a recording from 1963–64 of the same teller by D.A. MacDonald, held at the School of Scottish Studies, ref 42782 SA 1963.016. Several other versions of the MacVurich traditions are held and can be heard on www.tobarandulchais.co.uk.

Stories From South Uist also contains transcriptions of Angus MacLellan's retelling of Fingallian legends and some of the details relating to the allusions to Gailbhinn and Conan are taken from there. For a full and fluent retelling of Irish legends, see Mary Heaney, *Over Nine Waves* (Faber and Faber, London, 1994).

For a full collection of Gaelic maritime terminology and traditions see George MacLeod (of Great Bernera), *Muir is Tìr: Seòras Chaluim Sheòrais* (Acair, Stornoway, 2005).

Wit is much prized, as well as eloquence, in the oral culture of the Western Isles. Mrs Mary Ann MacInnes of Stilligarry was recorded by D.A. MacDonald quoting the response of one of the MacVurichs to the offer of a very meagre bowl of milk from Dunvegan of Skye and published in the School of Scottish Studies journal *Tocher* no. 57. He saw a fly floating in it and addressed it, 'Poor thing, you should never have drowned. You didn't need to swim. You could have waded through that.' (Quote paraphrased here.)

BENBECULA TO GRIMSAY

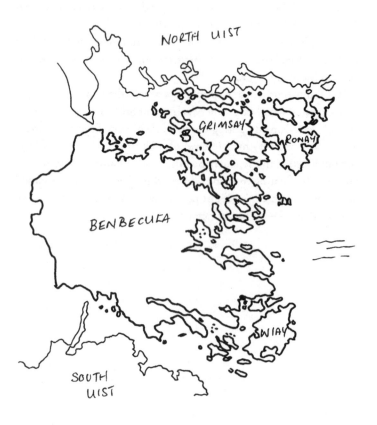

OUT THE WEST SIDE

If you're not used to seafaring you might have the idea that you'd feel more secure somehow in shallower water. It's really the other way round. Seas that have tumbled on for miles of open ocean become distorted when they are compressed in shallower areas. So fishing banks, where the sea bed rises steeply or where there is an underwater shelf of rock, will produce dangerous breaking waves. That's why the west side of the Outer Hebrides is still a very tricky place to navigate. Back in the days of open boats, it was no place to be caught out in a gale. There are also very few havens and very few bays which afford much shelter.

There are many shallows and sandbanks off the west side of the Uists. The colours of the water shift from a startling green to a deep kelp maroon to a muddy brownish grey. All give clues as to the changing depth under your keel. There is a song which celebrates the coming of the internal combustion engine, so a boat crossing to Heisker could head where it wanted, even against the wind.* But there is an earlier song of the boat where a crew think their number has been called.

The wind came up quickly and they reduced sail quickly. But the seas continued to rise. They towered up much higher than the gunnels of the boat and far higher than the tiller, at the stern. The only thing worse than the sight of the jagged waves was the crashing sound as energy was released from their breaking.

The waters piled so high above them that they could hardly make out the shore marks they needed to guide them into a safe landing. Everything went grey and white.

It came to the stage where even the skipper ceased to look astern. But it would not help, seeing what was coming at them. The Fair Weaver was known to thread the vessels under his command through the narrowest of channels. But this time he advised his crew to consider their lives thus far.

'Boys,' he said, 'we must look to our own salvation by thinking now of our own enemies. And there have been a few. Think now on the important things rather than on our possessions. I'm thinking of my own horse, that strong colt, the one that already knows his own way to the peat-banks. The one that can carry more than his share and shrug and snort, toss his white mane and tail and move at a pace I can hardly follow. I'll give the colt to the poor if we come through this.'

Donald Ard followed his example. 'It's not been the worst harvest I've known. But I'll give all my store of corn, all the grain, ready-threshed or no, the whole yield of the year, I'll give that to feed the poor.'

But it was a Morrison, young Alexander, the man with the tiller still in his hand, who put his other hand to the bailing scoop. 'Carry on with the good resolutions. I'll keep bailing in the meanwhile.'

And, of course, they all ceased trying to outdo each other with their promises and put a hand to casting the water out of the boat. She remained buoyant, just, and they all came through it. Which brings to mind a tradition from a very different culture, an Arabic proverb: 'Trust in God but tie your camel.'

The song is from am Bard Sgallach, *and there are no further verses to indicate that all these intended sacrifices were indeed carried out after the land was regained.*

References

* Dòmhnall Ruadh Chorùna (1887–1967) 'Motor Boat Heisker', in the collection *Dòmhnall Ruadh Choruna* (Comann Eachdraidh Uibhist a Tuath, North Uist, 1995). He is also represented in *an Tuil* (The Flood), ed. Ronald Black (Polygon, Edinburgh 1999).

Angus Campbell, am Bard Sgallach, was a tailor to the Clanranalds as well as a maker of songs. The above is suggested from the translation of one of these included in the MacDonald collection: http://digital.nls.uk/early-gaelic-book-collections/pageturner.cfm?id=76727688&mode=transcription.

There is also a very useful guide to the rhythms used in rowing songs from the same source:

> There were three kinds of boat-songs, *lorram mhor*, *Creagag*, and *lomarhhaigh*. The *lorram mhor* had no repetition of the chorus, and the air was somewhat slow. It was sung in large boats, after the land was left behind, and the rowers with a long and steady pull stretched themselves to the oars. *Creagag* is a quick, spirited song, adapted to a small boat among rocks (whence the name) and islands, where the oars require to be plied swiftly and lightly.
>
> The *lomarhhaigh* is sung by two rowers, verse about, and is properly sung extempore, each composing his verse, praising, or scolding, or arguing, as they proceed, and is intended to produce excitement in the rowers, lessen their toil, and provide a stimulus for their energies.

See the recordings of Mary Smith, from Galson, Isle of Lewis (Mairi Nic a' Ghobhainn), for examples of rowing songs. See also her book, *Orain mun t-Seòladh: Sheòl Mi 'n-Uiridh*, ISBN 9781900901505, Foillsichte le CLÀR, 2009.

THE DAY OF THE BLACK DOG

There was a shepherd on the Isle of Benbecula by the name of MacPhee. He worked for the laird there. He was responsible for more than one dog and he had quite a few men working under him. They would cover the whole of that island, every scrap of machair and moor, gathering and tending to all the flocks. Remember that this is before there was a causeway linking you to South Uist and another across the north ford. And long before there was an aerodrome. So it was very much an island in its own right.

At one time MacPhee kept both a dog and a bitch, his own animals, in addition to those he trained and ran for the laird. He could do little with the dog but the bitch was very handy. Folk asked him why he bothered to feed the heavy, black dog because it seemed to leave most of the running to the bitch. He had never been known even to bark. 'His time might come, yet,' MacPhee would say. They knew it was like an admission of defeat, to say that he had not managed to train that dog. Another time he would say, '*Thig latha chain duibh fhathast*.' The black dog will have its day.

Shearing time was the hardest work of all. The men used to gather the flocks at a place called Stangeval. There was a bothy there and they all just stayed the night, to save time in the morning. There were bunks for all and a stove and a place to boil up tea in one other crude room. This night MacPhee and his dogs were sitting up late by the fire when the rest of the exhausted men went through to their bunks. The shepherd never moved anywhere, even about the house, without his crook and he had his heavy outdoor plaid round his shoulders too. He was probably waiting up to let the dogs out the door one last time before they all slept.

He had called all his cousins to help get this job done, so there were a dozen men through the house. Every one of them had said much the same thing to his mate in the next bunk or to himself, before giving in to sleep, 'I could do with the arms of a woman around me now, rather than all this farting and snoring.'

MacPhee heard this said and called through that they might regret what they asked for. The fire was still on but it was getting very late, maybe gone midnight, when the door nudged open. MacPhee's head was falling on his shoulder but he saw there was not one but many visitors. He saw the whiteness of something like a pale face or a beak of bone under a dark cloth over the head of a figure that was certainly female. A line of dark women followed the first, without a sound, through the open door. MacPhee was powerless to move from his seat. The dog was silent as usual but even the bitch lay quiet and still, though her hackles were up.

It looked like he had nothing to fear because the line of women went through next door, without any hurry. But the last one sat down beside him on the bench. Still the dogs did not move, though their eyes were open. MacPhee didn't dare look too closely at the face of the figure who had joined him but he could see that something strange was happening. She had seemed very small when she first came through the door, maybe the height of a normal 6 year old. But now she'd grown in stature, seated beside him. He felt a chill as if she'd taken his warmth from him. His eyes were on the beaten earth of the floor. That's when he saw a trickle of damp coming from the room with the bunks. There was still not a sound to be heard.

'Well, I'd better be taking the dogs out,' he said to his uninvited guest.

'I don't think you're going anywhere at all,' came the reply.

But he said it was not only the dogs needed to pass water. 'You can hold on to the end of my plaid. I'll only need to go as far as the door.'

So she did that, but he took the other end and fastened it with his crook under the turfs that sat on the stones. He took off then, not waiting for a second chance. The black dog and the bitch were with him.

It was only a minute before a great howling noise came behind him and he knew they were on his trail, and very close too. There was only one thing he could do. He said to the black dog, 'If you've never run for me before, you'll run for me now. And take the bitch with you.'

He sent them back and the two obeyed at once, growling and chasing at whatever was coming behind them. He heard a mighty bark from the dog, for the very first time. MacPhee was breathless, jumping without his crook, from one tussock to the next. At last he saw the shape of his own house. His wife was in bed, of course, but he called for her help.

'Every basin, every bowl in the house. Every drop of milk from the byre. These dogs will have the thirst of hell on them.'

So the two rushed about, laying out all the bowls and basins, sloshing with milk. When all was done they closed the door behind them and slammed the wooden pin home.

There was a wailing and a snarling that went on for some time but all went still and quiet at last. I'm not saying they slept much, but the morning did come.

When MacPhee opened that door, sure enough the dog and the bitch were not very far away. But they were swollen up, like fishing-buoys of animal skin. And there was not one single hair left on either of their bodies.

I can't tell you if they recovered or not but they do say that a body of strong men went at once to the bothy out at Stangeval. When they went through the house, they found twelve bodies, cold and pale but without the sign of a wound on any. They say the sharp beaks must have gone through like needles and the blood drawn from them that way. I can tell you what they call that hut, out on the moor. That's 'One-night Sheiling', because no one since has ever stayed there for more than one. That's *Àirigh na h-Aon Oidhce*.

References

Retold from the story recorded from Peter MacCormick, Benbecula, by Angus John MacDonald. He was also recorded by Calum MacLean in the 1940s and '50s. See full notes after tale no. 61 in Bruford and MacDonald. This telling also has details from the transcription of the story from one Angus MacKinnon, as heard from his mother. This was made by Alexander Carmichael in 1871 and can be found in the online archive of the Carmichael Watson project (Coll – 97/ CW119/20).

The tale is also associated with Tiree and an earlier transcription, from Donald Cameron, Ruaig, Tiree, with a full introduction, was published by the Revd J.G. Campbell in *West Highland Tales*, in 1863. See http://www.angelfire.com/dragon2/leavesandtrees/cailleach/ blackdog.html.

You can hear no less than seven recorded versions of the tale on www.tobarandualchais.co.uk (Kist o Riches, from the archive of the School of Scottish Studies). The Morrison manuscript also has several tales of chases through the night and the motif of the dog losing its hair also appears. Compare the tale on p. 83, where a phantom horse makes the chase. *Tocher*, no. 57, prints, in parallel text Gaelic and English, a very similar story from Neil Gillies, of Barra, recorded by D.A. MacDonald.

A Way of Taking Herring

The tailor used to be an itinerant worker. He would take his shears and his needles and threads in a pack and move from house to house in the search for work. Folk would take him in and give him his board, as part of his wages. He would make up clothes or coverings for them, often from material woven by them from the wool of their own sheep. They would be glad of his conversation as well as his workmanship. Being a fellow who moved around so much, he'd likely have plenty of stories. Everyone wanted to hear something new, once in a while.

One time such a tailor, and a very good one by all accounts, was visiting the island of Grimsay at the east side of Benbecula. There is

a decent harbour at Kallin and the Grimsay folk are well known for boatbuilding as well as being very handy fisherfolk. They often take their strong vessels through the ford and out west to Heisker, to work the rich lobster grounds. Maybe that's why the tailor thought nothing of it when his lady host, who seemed to be living on her own, produced fresh herring for his breakfast, every morning.

There's few things tastier than a crisp, firm herring, coated in browned oatmeal. 'You can cook that for me every morning, if you can find them,' he said.

But to his surprise, it was the same thing at the next house, which was also run by a lady who seemed to be on her own. But he really did think it strange when the same thing happened at the third. He was by no means sick of herring yet. He could eat them every day, but he was beginning to wonder where they were all coming from. He asked this third woman where they were getting all that fresh fish. Every scale was intact and the colours of the rainbow were present in the silver.

'Oh, we've no problem in finding them,' she said. The three of them were all a bit beyond the first flush of youth so the tailor thought they must have relations who caught the herring.

But, since tailors are naturally curious creatures, he sat up late one night. All his hosts seemed to be very anxious to see that he got to his bed at an early hour. 'You've plenty to do in the morning,' one would say. 'It's a short enough night,' the next one said. And so on.

But at the third house he said he'd finished sewing every stitch they'd set out for him and he'd be away home in the morning. It was a long way and he didn't dare sleep in, so he'd just stay awake and that would be that. The woman of the house did her best to talk him out of that idea but soon she saw there was no arguing with him.

'Well, seen as you're set on staying up, you might as well make yourself useful. But you mustn't breathe a word to anyone.'

He swore he would not, and so was taken along on the fishing expedition. He was not surprised to see that the three old souls met up when the rest of the village was sound asleep. The other two were annoyed to see the tailor in their company but his present host persuaded them he could be trusted. He was away next day, anyway. Sure enough they could do with another hand.

They led him to the shore and lifted a rock or two to reveal their gear, hidden away. There was nothing but three wide sieves – the sort you'd use to sift stones from soil – and three coils of hand-made heather rope. The tailor's eyes near popped out of his head when he saw each of the old woman stand on a sieve. In turn, each said a rhyme that was like a foreign language to him. Then the three of them were out, afloat in the bay. They were all roped together, each one joined up. His job was to hold the end of the loop of rope and do nothing till he was told to. Then he'd to pull the whole lot in. He'd see there would be a herring caught by the gills in every stalk of heather.

The spells were said and there was a glint of herring in the water. The moon came out and things were going very well until the tailor got a bit excited and without thinking said the usual thing, 'In the name of the Lord, fish well.'

Each of the three sieves went down like a stone and the three women were in the water splashing and choking. The tailor pulled on the rope for all he was worth. He couldn't leave them to drown and the three bedraggled creatures came coughing and cursing to the shore.

He didn't stay around to hear what they had to say to him then, but took to the path over the hill at once, to begin his journey back home. He didn't care for his scissors or his pack. He was thankful to escape from these strange happenings. It was a long enough journey but he was in his own house before dawn and very glad of it. But he'd have one more story to tell at the next house he was asked to visit, bringing his skills.

References
No. 81, from Peter Morrison, Grimsay, in Bruford and MacDonald. Angus MacLellan told a version where the three women turn into rats once the tailor makes a blessing. In turn this suggests a religious tradition, recorded by Father Allan MacDonald, where grain, left in a chest by a selfish woman who refuses to help a stranger, turns into rats, a previously unknown animal.

THREADS OF THREE COLOURS

In the month of February, in the year of 1906, a man from the parish of Benbecula made the crossing to the island of Grimsay, to buy a horse. The Grimsay people had a good name for breeding horses and he was keen to look over some of their stock.

As he was passing a croft he saw a very good example, close to the road, and praised it out loud. He had not walked on far when the same animal fell to the ground. It was in agony. The owner came rushing out. He'd seen the stranger passing and recognised him as a man they claimed had the evil eye on him. Who knows why a man would do that? Maybe he also bred horses and was attacking the competition.

So the owner went at a run to a neighbour's house. She was also known to have special powers but she used them for healing and for good. When she heard the story she said she knew what to do.

Her neighbour, the owner of the stricken horse, saw her put three threads, all of different colours, to her teeth and twist them into a cord. She did this three times so there were three lengths of cord, all of them three-ply. She said he was to tie these, one after the other, round the root of the horse's tail and at the same time invoke the names of the Father, the Son and the Holy Spirit.

He took these and hurried back down the crofts to the poor beast, which was still on the ground. He did exactly as he'd been instructed. As soon as he'd completed the third tie and said the invocation for the third time, the beast stirred. It was on its feet in minutes. It shook itself and then lowered its head to graze and seemed none the worse for the attack.

The owner went at once to thank that woman who had helped. She told him that she had inherited her gift from her late father. He had been a good man of few words but many prayers. The procedure would leave her exhausted for some days. She always needed to rest for a good period afterwards. That woman was always respected and loved throughout the whole of the island of Grimsay, and she was also known a lot further afar than that.

References
Retold from reported tradition, collected by Alexander Carmichael, *Carmina Gadelica* (Oliver & Boyd, Edinburgh, 1954, p. 166).

NORTH UIST AND
OUTLYING ISLANDS

THE BEACHCOMBER

It will be no surprise to hear that shipwrecks were all too common on the west side of the Uists. If a vessel was driven in close, there were few places to run and she would be pounded on the banks or on the reefs. Usually, all those aboard perished. It was very rare to get a line out to a stricken ship in those days. In later days, a hawser, which could carry a breeches-buoy for rescue, could be taken out by means of a messenger-line, propelled by rocket. In the twentieth century, the largest number of survivors ever rescued by breeches-buoy came ashore from the Clan MacQuarry, which grounded on the west side of North Lewis. But this story is set long before that and on the coastline of North Uist.

There are still rich strips of fertile machair close to these shores. Back in time, one major farm was divided into no less than fourteen holdings. It was not a very prosperous living for so many. Crofters would look to the shores for anything to supplement what they could get from the soil. It was quite common to find the flotsam and jetsam from a stricken vessel. Much more rare to find laggan – gear or goods, cast but buoyed with the hope of eventual recovery. There might be a small cask of butter. A cask of rum was not unknown. Any timber was precious and prized. You could hardly build a roof without it.

But one man searched the shores to the point of obsession. On the wildest night, he'd be drenched and shivering, but still raking amongst the weed and foam for any finds. He lived alone and his simple home was full of items salvaged from the losses of others. But he never seemed to find anything really valuable.

At last his nephew thought he might try to prevent his uncle finding an early death by pneumonia, from his habit of walking out in storms. First he said his piece on how the goods of this world were worthless in comparison to companionship. The older man was missing many a good song and story, as well as readings from The Book, when he was out alone on the shores. But nothing he said made any difference. The old fellow always complained that very little came his way compared to the finds of his neighbours.

So this is what the nephew did. One day, after a fierce blast from the west, he made sure he had his best brogues on as he passed by his uncle's house. He stopped to pass the time of day now that a calm had come. The uncle had, of course, been out the night before but found very little. Then his eyes fell on his nephew's fine footwear. 'These weren't made in our village,' he said.

'No they were not. I found them on a poor corpse which came ashore last night.' And he named a shore which he knew would not be the one his uncle haunted.

'We could do nothing for that poor soul except bury him. But at least these will not go to waste.'

Sure enough, the uncle was out that very evening, sifting through the weed piled at the shore his nephew had named. He came across a pair of prosperous looking legs, jutting out from a pile of debris. The corpse was wearing a pair of shoes as fine as those he'd seen that day. He put a hand to one, in delight. But the leg gave a kick which struck the old fellow in the jaw. He jumped three feet in the air.

Then the nephew showed himself, laughing away, now that his trap had been sprung. It was only his uncle's pride that was seriously hurt. The younger man admitted he'd paid for these same shoes, himself, last time he was in Glasgow. 'I hope you'll remember the shock you got tonight and put your mind on other things,' he said to his uncle.

But they say the incident was forgotten within a few months and the elder man was back at his old habits.

References
Retold from the Morrison manuscript, no. 149, 'Dead Men's Shoes'. It invites comparison with a tale from Fetlar, Shetland, from Jamsie Laurenson, retold by Lawrence Tulloch, author of *Shetland Folk Tales*, in this series. The central imagery is again a fine pair of boots on a dead man.

AN ELOPEMENT

You'll have heard tell how the MacDonald Estates, in the Uists, fell into decline. Some say it was gambling and some say it was poor harvests and hard winters so there was not enough hay to feed the cattle. Whether it was mismanagement or bad luck, the effect was the same on the poor tenants. An advocate from Aberdeen was called in as commissioner and this fellow, by the name of Cooper, was known to be pitiless.

His decrees for removals led to the clearances at Sollas. He must have had some sort of feelings in him, though. They say he fell for Jessie MacDonald, a daughter of James Thomas MacDonald of Balrananald. His bid for her hand was very much welcomed by Jessie's parents. It was better to have a man like that as an ally than an enemy. The only difficulty was the same one that's in most of the songs. Her heart was already given to one Donald of Monkstadt. To add to the insult, Donald had been the former estate factor but he had been replaced because they said he was too lenient with the tenants for these hard times.

He was also an able fellow, not short of courage, but he was the younger son in a Skye family which had also suffered in the harder times. So he was no great prospect.

Jessie was put under unbearable pressure. It was not that she was forced, but she felt she could not deny her parents this hope of a change in their fortunes. Then maybe she saw for herself the suffering caused by Patrick Cooper. It's a terrible sight, the blackened stone walls where a roof had recently sheltered a family. The keening of folk boarding a crowded emigrant ship, knowing that some will not survive the crossing.

She got a message to the man she loved, Donald of Monkstad: 'We must be off this night. You had better not come for me till half past eleven.'

Donald did get hold of a small vessel. He could depend on support from his own kin and friends even though they were bound to face the wrath of those whose plans were thwarted. This craft was open to the elements but seaworthy and driven by a single but powerful lugsail. But this was not a night you would choose to go to sea. The crossing to Skye can be benign but the Little Minch can change its mood very quickly. This song could so easily have been one of the many hard laments with imagery of sodden canvas and a mast in splinters.

They boarded safely and his crew did their best to point that vessel for his home island, where he had family who would take them in. But the wind and the seas decided otherwise. The wind went to the south-east and rose till it screamed. They had little option but to run for the shelter of Rodel. Donald knew not to risk the open seaward entrance and knew not to attempt the rocky shallows even though you could see the signs of light and warmth around the pier, through the gap. He held her till they were well into Loch Rodel and the safer, tidal entrance opened up.

They were still on the flooding tide, past the halfway mark, so they could sail the skiff into the safe pool. There was now no option but to give Jessie over to the protection of her kinsman, John Robertson MacDonald, tacksman at Rodel. He did take her in but threw her Skyeman out. He knew all too well that the family needed stronger financial alliances to rebuild their estates.

The settlement of Rodel is known for the solid architecture of its church. At that time its piers and buildings, of stone and slate, also showed that a healthy trade had left some of its profits in the place.

But, sure enough, Cooper and his henchmen came looking for the Skyeman and the fiancée he had reclaimed. Cooper was not going to be cheated. But Donald of Monkstadt gathered his own support and had the vessel ready for sea again. There was a struggle, but the song doesn't give us many details:

Ne'er was seen such hurly-burly,
Climbing and descending stairs.
Locks were broken, doors burst open,
Got her out in spite of all.

Then cried out the Bailie Cooper,
Loaded pistol in his hand,
First in English then in Gaelic:
'Who is he?' And '*Co sud ann.*'

We only know that a gun was shown but the fists and sticks of Donald and his kinsmen disarmed the stronger force before any harm could be done.

By this time the wind had veered to the south-west and the lovers again took to sea before the forces against them could regather. They had more friends at Gairloch. And this time the crossing went as they hoped. They lost no time, on arrival, in making the few arrangements they needed. There was no fuss and no feasting but they were legally married. Donald and Jessie knew enough of the world to be sure that they could not fight the power held by the advocate and his financial allies.

They took their passage to make a new life for themselves. Donald was steeped in farming and that knowledge would serve them wherever they were granted land. You won't be surprised to find that their acres, near Queensland, Australia, were called Balranald. But you'd be wrong if you thought that was them settled and safe.

There were desperate characters in that land too. When her husband rode out to see to the business of the flourishing farm, Jessie was kidnapped by a bushranger. But she had surely chosen the right man. Her Skyeman was as handy on a horse as he was with a skiff. He rode out to attack the outlaw's camp and shot his man dead. Jessie came home to their own Balranald unhurt and as the records show, and the song celebrates, they lived to a very good age in the new land.

References

Retold from a summary of the song in Donald A. Fergusson (ed.), *From the Farthest Hebrides* (Macmillan, London, 1978, p. 160). See also Bill Lawson's retelling in *Harris in History and Legend* (John Donald, Edinburgh, 2002 p. 72). Statements made to the Napier commission by supporters of Donald of Monkstadt counterpoint the romance of this apparently true story.

This is another fine example of how the essence of a tale, probably based on historical events, is captured in a much-travelled song, but less usual in its happy ending. It takes us close to the geography in the great lament 'Ailean Duinn', existing in many versions, including the Uist waulking song recorded by Margaret Fay Shaw (See *Folksongs and Folklore of South Uist*, 2nd edn, Oxford University Press, Oxford).

BLACK JOHN

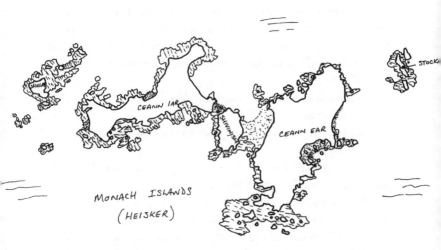

Most people think of the devastating raids from the sea as the work of Viking marauders but there is a whole history of clan battles, raids and counter-raids the long length of the Outer Hebrides. The Harris MacLeods would forage into the territory of the Clanranalds in the Uists. Once, a band from the north, in a fast and seaworthy vessel, raided and pillaged a coastal village on the west side of North Uist. But times had been poor and the Harrismen were not yet satisfied. They wanted to get out to Heisker, in the Monach islands. These were known to be very fertile ground. At that time there were a good many families living there and it was known as a good place for rearing cattle. They were sure to carry off a carcass or two.

But first they had to reach it. The Sound is full of shallows and reefs and the approaches into the anchorages out there are known to be tricky. They needed a pilot. So they asked who had a good knowledge of the route to Heisker and everyone said Black John was the man. He was not exactly keen. He knew he'd be bringing a curse out to these peaceful islands, but he did not have a lot of choice in the matter.

The Harris skipper was nervous and kept asking for the names of the points and reefs they passed. John was stationed at the stern with him and kept up his commentary on the marks and transits, pointing which way to take through the breaking waters. The weather was not that great to start with but it grew worse as they came close. A squall of hard sleet and hail hit them and they could hardly see what was in front of them.

'Do you still know where we are?' the skipper said.

'I do', says Black John.

'Well you just remember, if we go down you'll go down with us.'

'Aye,' says John.

When they could hear the waves breaking on the rocks, they could just make out one dark point, jutting out.

'Make for that one,' John said, 'but sail as close as you possibly can. There's deep water right up close but a reef further out.'

So the Harris skipper did exactly that, taking her in close. 'I'll go forward now,' says John. 'You'll be more confident if I take the lookout and point the way, from the bow.'

They allowed him to do that and he took his place, right at the tack of the sail. When they were a hair's breadth from the point, he put a hand on the taut front edge of the sail, the luff, as they call it, and that helped him spring ashore. The boat sailed on past the point, but not for long. There was a crash and the harsh sound of splintering timber. Black John watched from his secure stance on the land.

Below him the vessel was breaking up and the raiders were meeting their fate in the cold and crashing waters.

'You never asked me the name of this point,' he shouted down to the last of them. 'I don't know what it was called before but it will be called *Rubha nam Marbh* from now on.'

You won't be surprised to learn that the name means 'The Point of Death'.

The people of Heisker knew that John had done them a great service. They looked after him so well that soon he had his own house and croft and a wife as well. I don't believe he ever returned to the mainland but he made a good living for himself out there.

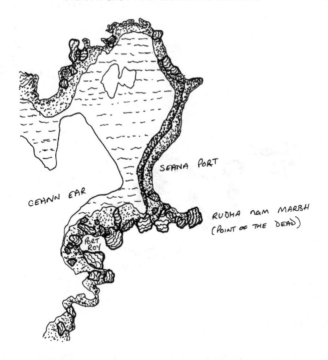

References

I knew of this tradition from several conversations crewing traditional boats, from Lewis to the Uists. I then came across the taut version, transcribed and translated from Angus MacKenzie by D.A. MacDonald. It is no. 56 in Bruford and MacDonald and the associated notes are detailed.

Later, I was lucky enough to hear and record the story and others, in both Gaelic and English, from Angus 'Moy' MacDonald at the old schoolhouse on Heisker, which he attended as a boy. Angus joined our team aboard the Berneray community boat *Sealladh* for the voyage out and back. A transcription of his telling is included in my book on voyaging through traditional stories, *Waypoints* (unpublished to date), but the one above is my own retelling, based on several versions.

For video footage of sailing through the landscape of Uist songs, see a collaboration with Andy MacKinnon (Uistfilm) for Taigh Chearsabhagh – *confluence,* 2007: http://vimeo.com/16023887.

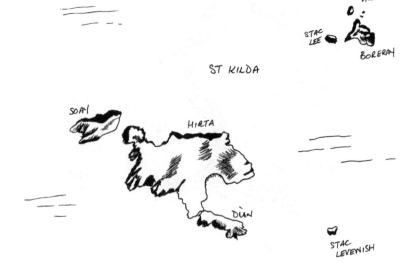

A Boat Race

There was not much interest in the ownership of Hirta and the other islands which make up the St Kilda group until some of its produce came into demand. Seabirds of different species were the mainstay of the diet on that island, 40 miles out from the western approach to the Sound of Harris. The feathers were bagged and stored once someone discovered that they rivalled the down of the eider for warmth. Thus a rent could be paid. But Hirta was claimed by both the MacDonalds of Uist and the MacLeods of Harris.

Usually the clans would resort to raids and battles to settle disputes but this time the rival lairds agreed to a different proposition. Two keels were to be laid, on identical lines. Two vessels were built, to the same dimensions, with the same number and type of oars and the same rig. The sails were sewn at the same time, from matching cloth. Even after that, lots were drawn so each vessel flew a different banner. The race would begin when the rocky islet of Coppay was left astern and end when one of the chiefs could put his hand on Hirta (*Hiort*), some 40 sea miles to the west.

When the wind was favourable the vessels skipped over the waves and when it fell light or contrary the oars were deployed. All the men put their backs into it. It was their honour, more than the prize, which would go to their chief.

First, one of the like boats would nudge into a slight lead, and then an easing of the sheet or a fine adjustment of the halyard would give the other an advantage. There was not a boat length between them as the land fell from sight to the east and nothing but a high cloud could be seen in the west.

The high ground of Boreray came up first but the prows were aimed to the south of that, where Village Bay provides some shelter so long as the wind is not from the east. Soon the outlying reef of Levenish could be seen, and inside it the current on the waters which flood and ebb between the islands.

MacDonald read the signs on the water best. He took his vessel in close to catch an eddy which gave them an extra knot or so of speed. And that was enough. MacLeod was slow to respond. The oars were

out and his men were giving their all and keeping in time but they were now two boat lengths astern. The shore of Hirta was just out of reach – but it could have been 100 sea miles away.

That's when the MacLeod skipper put his own left hand to the bottom boards. He had one of his men swing the ship's axe – you carried one in case a spar or sail had to come down in a hurry. 'Put my hand to that Island,' he said to his most trusted man. Then he reached for a cloth to staunch the flow of blood.

The object made a high curve through the air and struck a stone on Hirta the moment before the MacDonald prow hit the shingle. Remember the terms: 'Whosoever shall put a hand to Hirta first shall be deemed the winner and therefore the owner of that island.'

And that's why the St Kilda islands were the responsibility of the MacLeods for many years to come.

References

Thanks to Donald Smith (Director of the Scottish Storytelling Centre) for pointing out that a similar story is told of Colum Cille racing Moluag to claim Lismore, except that only a finger was sacrificed in that case, to win jurisdiction for Moluag. *The Bloody Hand of Ulster,* another version of the tale, is also very close to one told in the Rhineland of Germany.

I was brought up with this story, though the version in the Morrison manuscript has the rule that whoever sets fire on the island takes it. A torch is thrown to win the race. Bill Lawson's version in *Harris in History and Legend* also has the severed hand.

HOLDING TOGETHER

Most of the work needed to sustain the communities of the Outer Hebrides was done as a community. It wasn't only on Hirta. People gathered to discuss the priorities of the day on Scarp and no doubt on Taransay and Mingulay and probably in most of the villages throughout the islands. Whether fishing or fowling, sowing or reaping, much of the work could only be done if folk pulled together.

The St Kildans would set a longline or two, but usually when they were on their way to land men on the cliffs. Winds sweep down from the heights of the gabbro rock with no warning, so you can understand that these people did not want the obligation of taking to the sea to fish for their living. The women, too, would do their share of snaring puffins and fulmars on the lower slopes.

That's why the most valuable thing in St Kildan society was a rope rather than a cow. And that's why there was a tradition of a man proving he had the balance and courage needed on the cliffs to provide for his new wife and the family they might rear.

There is a story that one time two men went together to the cliffs to catch the dark sentinels which make a very fine soup or stew – the cormorant or shag. One braced himself, with feet out wide, at the top and one went over the edge, feet to the rock, as he descended.

The climber was able to trap a good number. Soon there was a huddle of dark shapes hanging from his belt.

'I think you've enough for the two of us now,' the man at the top called down.

'Let every man take his own cormorant from the cliff,' came the reply.

'If that's how it is, let every man hold his own rope,' said the man at the top as he let it go.

You can see the image of a man in the sea, with the dark shapes of long-necked birds, all out in a ring of death from his waist.

Talking of images, here's another one.

The party of fowlers were landed on Stac Biorach in the Sound of Soay. That rock was named after the smoothest thing there is – that spine at the dorsal fin of a spur-dog – and that's what it looks like. There was a particular hold, made with the thumb and then a spring to the next one. The lead climber had to complete that manoeuvre to set the rope in place. But, this day, the cliff-men were only just in position when they saw an image in the water beneath them.

It was a body in the sea. It was floating face-down and it was wearing the greyish plaid that most of them wore. But they were all accounted for. As they watched, a black-backed gull landed on the corpse and began to peck at its neck. I'm sure they made an effort to recover that body, but it disappeared from sight almost at once. They were looking to each other, hardly daring to ask if they'd all indeed seen the same thing.

But they'd managed to get that far and it might be long enough before conditions would let the boat drop them there again. So they continued the climb. Within minutes there was a fall. When they looked down they all recognised what they'd seen before, exactly the same sight. Except that now they could also see that one of their number was missing.

References
The first tradition is included in Margaret Fay Shaw's *Folksongs and Folklore of South Uist*, p. 60, ascribed to Seonaid Caimbeul, as recorded by Margaret's husband, John Lorne Campbell.

The key Gaelic phrase is '*Biodh a ch-uile duine toirt sgairbh a creig dha fhein.*' The second is reported by Charles MacLean in his *Island on the Edge of the World* (Tom Stacey, London, 1972) but there is no note of the original source.

I have retold this story while free-climbing a low pitch in 'the tunnel' at Glen Bay, Hirta, within sight of Soay, so the tension of holding is in the voice. This was filmed by Matt Wainwright, on the same voyage aboard *Song of the Whale* (see http://www.capefarewell. com/2011expedition/2011/08/02/blue-bonnets/). This was part of the Scottish Islands project by Cape Farewell, an organisation which draws attention to issues of climate change. For me, this story, like many traditional island tales, has at its heart a sense of our vulnerability. And of our essential interdependence. Arguably our whole survival as a species on this planet is now also on a knife-edge. But we're not so aware of it, in daily life.

5

Harris and Outlying Islands

MEALASTA

SCARP

HUSHINISH

NORTH
HARRIS

SOUND OF SHIANT

TARANSAY

SOUND OF TARANSAY

SOUTH
HARRIS

SOUND OF HARRIS

ENSAY

BERNERAY

SOUTH
UIST

THE COWHIDE

I'm going to tell you about something that happened in a simple thatched dwelling like any other. There was nothing special about it.

Every house at that time had a partition in it, just a hint of a separation between the section where the people lived and where the animals were housed. Now the family that lived here killed their cow when it grew old. They would waste nothing in these days. Folk used to dry the hide to make garments and boots and all sorts of things out of it, even laces for their shoes. In this house, the cow's hide was hung over the partition.

There was one girl living in the house with her father and mother. She was very beautiful and she used to go to the hill with the cattle every day. She'd return on her own and then go out again in the evening to bring the beasts home.

Once she met a young lad on the hill. She had never seen this fellow in the village and she had no idea who he belonged to. But she was sure she had never seen anyone as handsome. He would walk with her till she was nearly home and then take his leave. Then he would tilt his head a bit, by way of a leave-taking, and he'd be off to where he'd come from.

That went on for six months. She was deeply in love with the lad but she wondered why he never said a word. She also wondered why no one else who lived close had ever seen him before. She asked all around but no one could say who his people were.

The poor girl was getting anxious. At last she went to an old tinker woman who lived down the glen, a bit apart from the village. She gave a nod. The story made sense to her and she knew just what to do.

'My dear, as soon as you reach home again, take a strand from the tail of the cowhide you've got hanging up in the house. Wash it and clean it and then you can make it into one long plait. Then you must lay it aside. I can tell you for sure, it won't be long before that lad will ask you for a lock of your hair. Give him the plait you've made from the cow's tail. On no account let him have anything of your own.'

Sure enough, it wasn't long before the lad made a sign that he was anxious to get a lock of her own hair. She told him she'd bring it back out of the house with her, when she'd come out again, to go and fetch the cattle. That's what she did but you know what she handed over to him.

Safe back in the house, her father was 'taking the books', as we say – holding family worship – close to midnight. When the clock struck, the hide they'd hung over the partition began to hop. Soon it was skipping and moving like a mad thing.

Her father darted over to swing the door open and out it went. He went out after it and called on his neighbours and their lads. They all chased it, with horses, dogs and all. But they couldn't gain on that thing until it reached the spot they call *Cnoc an t-Sìthein*.

The cowhide that had come alive stopped there and vanished from sight. And they never did find that skin again or any sign of it. They knew then they'd been well-advised. If that girl had given her own hair she would have been out that same door and they would never have set eyes on her again.

References
Mrs Katherine Dix, Berneray, Harris, recorded by Ian Paterson SA1968/184.B6. Translation reprinted in Bruford and MacDonald, no. 3a. The editors place it with a similar tale from Shetland but there are several other variants and similar traditions.

MATTERS OF JUSTICE

They say that an old woman in Harris went to all the trouble of boiling a pot of water just so she could pour the lot on the grave of a man from a rival clan. She had not been able to scald the tenant of that six feet of land when he was still on the top of the ground so she took her chance when he was under it.

There were occasional signs of a more humane spirit, even in the days of raiding and feuding. A challenge was put out to the honour of the MacLeods of Harris from a MacAulay of Brenish in Uig, very close to the Harris border. A small man with the name of Angus was sent to represent the MacLeods. 'Thanks for turning out today,' this unlikely champion said to the MacAulay hero. This provoked the heavier and stronger-looking man and he gave a very good account of himself. But in the end it was the smaller man who closed in and quite gently cut a button from the MacAulay's shirt, just below his throat. No blood was drawn.

'Will that do the business?' he asked.

In his wisdom, MacAulay assented.

'Well, you know now you've a MacLeod in front of you,' the small man said, 'though you've not yet met the chief.'

They say this same man was the last of the clan MacLeod to be entombed at Rodel Church. They also say that no one ever got the better of him when long blades were drawn.

Sometimes the rival clans were caught up in terrible crimes, committed by renegade members. There was an inevitable conflict between clan loyalty and justice.

One Malcolm MacDonald, described as 'a turbulent, wild man', lived on his own in the Bays of Harris. Folk gave him a wide berth but one time his neighbour, a Morrison, was missing a cow. He'd searched the high ground and the low before he thought of asking his neighbour if he'd seen any sign of her.

'Half your cow was boiled for my dinner and the rest could make our breakfast in the morning.' MacDonald held out a bone with meat on it. Morrison tried to placate this unpredictable man, knowing he was in danger. But that did not save him. He was a witness to a capital crime and so was slain in cold blood. This was in Drinishader, on the rocky east side of Harris, and there is no depth of soil there to hide a body.

First, MacDonald severed the head from the corpse, I suppose to make it more difficult to identify if it was ever found. Then he tied up the remains in the hide of the slaughtered beast. This was cast into the sea to let the waves and the tides have their effect. But the evidence was washed up on the Isle of Scalpay, not very far away. Headless corpse or no, a man of dubious reputation lived close to a missing cow and a missing man.

MacDonald heard that the Morrisons were set on bringing him to justice and escaped across to Skye, a stronghold of his own people. There he gave his own slant on events. His chief, MacDonald of Duntulm, thought it best to protect this man, whether he believed his story or not. A hanging would bring disgrace to the whole clan. 'I will keep you for seven years,' he said. 'You can take your place alongside my own herdsman, high up in the glen where no one else is likely to meet you.'

But the brothers of the murdered Morrison also crossed the Little Minch. They were canny in their enquiries. Soon they learned that the fugitive would spend his days on a high lookout post and his nights in the herdsman's cottage. Day or night, he would always have a keen dagger to hand. The Morrisons met the herdsman.

'Your chief has had enough of that man who crossed over from Harris.'

'I'm pleased to hear that because I'm sick of him, myself.'

They persuaded the unsuspecting herdsman to help part the dangerous man from his weapon. He should kill a goat and then say he needed a good blade to cut off a leg of it for their supper. When the herdsman showed that knife at a window, the Morrisons would come to take the murderer.

When MacDonald came back from his outpost he went to chop some wood to liven up the fire. But the axe was nowhere to be found. Then the herdsman asked him for a few minutes' use of his blade to sever a leg from the goat. First MacDonald said no, and then the thought of roast meat got the better of his judgement and he handed it over.

That's how he was taken and bound as a prisoner. But the Morrisons were decent enough to tell the herdsman that they had tricked him and his chief knew nothing of this. That's why the herdsman thought it wiser to go at a run to MacDonald of Duntulm and tell him his kinsman had been taken.

A dozen armed men overtook the Morrisons and their prisoner was reclaimed. On returning to Harris, they appealed to their own laird, who happened to be married to a daughter of MacDonald of Duntulm. The Morrison chief took up the cause. If the guilty man was not handed back, this would be taken as an insult to all his people.

The letter was not exactly moderate in its terms. 'Even though you are my father-in-law the joined forces of all our kin in Harris will not rest until we have filled a hood with the teeth of the men who have sheltered the criminal.'

That did the trick and the prisoner was sent back to Dunvegan and onward to Rodel in Harris. He kept his appointment with the rope and his body was left to swing on the gibbet.

The times were changing. A guilty man could not always be protected by his chief. As another man told it, 'A wind hit the poor bones.' A traveller spoke to the terrible sight, 'You earned your fate. The speed of your own hand brought you to this place.'

Sometimes, the plunder was carried out by well-organised expeditions.

One crew of warriors from Lewis, to the north, navigated the Kyles of Scarp to make a landfall by the township of Hushinish on the west side of North Harris. If there was an insult or a wrong behind this attack, the details are lost to us now. The killing started as soon as their feet hit the land and did not stop till there was no sign of one man from that village left alive. But one did indeed save himself because he was a boatbuilder, working in a sawpit, below the level of the raised banks at the shore. He kept himself hidden and so overheard one of the raiders say that they would strike the island of Taransay next.

As soon as the Lewis raiders left, the survivor put his own small vessel to sea and crossed the few miles, southward to Taransay. He landed to find that the folk had already gathered for a wedding. He gave his warning and the Taransay men prepared themselves for battle. They were indeed ready when the raiders crept over a mound, thinking they had the benefit of surprise.

At the end of it all there was only one of the raiding party left standing. He took to the sea and swam for his life. It's a considerable distance across the Sound of Taransay but the islanders did not want to let even one of the raiders escape. The bow was still a weapon of choice then and the Taransay men sent a rain of thudding arrows that you'd think none could survive. But this fugitive, wounded though he was, landed on a skerry and gulped in air. He continued on and gained the Harris shore. Then he hobbled from the machair and was lost to sight.

The years went by till one time the people of Taransay went north into Lewis, to Glen Miavaig, taking their cattle to winter pasture. Somehow their best horse went missing along that way. Days and weeks passed with no news of it. But after some months, when they were back at home, what should they hear but that the very horse had been sighted, alive, right up in North Lewis, in the district of Ness. Their own best-bred stock had distinguishing marks.

They could not leave it at that. One of their number was sent on the long journey to take a closer look. At last he reached the district of Habost. It was the Taransay horse all right, but he never let on that he knew anything about it and so was taken in to the crofthouse, according to the laws of hospitality. It turned out that these were Morrisons. In their home area, they were now respected people and this was the household of one known as 'the brieve' – he had a role in carrying out affairs of justice in this territory. That was an irony if ever there was one.

Drams were taken. But when the rest were at last off to their beds, the man of the house and his guest remained at the fire. The Lewisman was in some discomfort and stood close to the blazing peat, warming the backs of his legs and ankles. The guest looked at the host's legs and saw the signs of wounds, healed over.

'I don't think you got these scars by sitting at the fire.'

'No, I did not, and I wouldn't be surprised if your own hand fired some of the arrows. I had eight of them in me and I still escaped with my life. That was my only visit to Taransay.'

Surprise turned to shock and then became fear. But the brieve had not yet finished saying his piece. 'I can see you're scared but there's no need of that now. I'm a mortal man all right, just a lucky one. If you hadn't done that to us, we'd have done it to you.'

When the Taransay man took his leave in the morning, he took their own horse home with him, and another fine one to keep it company.

References

This is not a translation but a free retelling of versions of well-known tales which cross the borders of Lewis and Harris. It is very much based on the grouping of clan legends as arranged by the Reverend Calum MacLean and broadcast on BBC Radio. See also *Am Measg Nam Bodach, Calum Macgilleathain* (an Comunn Gaidhealach, Glaschu, 1938). I have spliced in some remembered details from my uncle Kenneth Murdo Smith's storytelling, passed on from my grandfather Murdo Finlay Smith.

The story of the escape from Taransay is also sketched in Bill Lawson, *Lewis: in History and Legend* (Birlinn, Edinburgh, 2008, p. 41), which quotes from a Revd William Matheson in a letter to the *Stornoway Gazette*. The Morrison manuscript (p. 95) provided more of the detail of the tale of the felon of Drinishader. There are many similar tales of feuds and battles. Morrison also stresses the importance of the archer, as in his tale of the slaying of the last water horse in the Uig district (p. 79).

Donald J. MacLeod, a retired policeman living in Aberdeen, who has published his own memories of crossing between Scarp and the Uig mainland (The Islands Book Trust) generously allowed me to record him describing the work of the itinerant boatbuilders of Uig, who would travel from township to township. He did suggest that some of these stout men left more than boats in the villages.

I am also greatly indebted to the late Ewan MacRae, the last person resident on Taransay. He ferried me across the changeable Sound to Bayble and to Uidhe many times when I used to help organise maintenance of the bothy at Uidhe. I never heard similar historical tales from Ewan but I did gain some sense of the strength of the community which survived on that island for so long and a sense of its placement, looking north to the rampart of the North Harris hills.

Song of the Whale, chartered by Cape Farewell, visited Taransay, in 2011, where I was reminded of Ewan's gentle spirit. See http://www.capefarewell.com/2011expedition/2011/08/03/tarasaigh.

ANNA CAMPBELL

There was a tacksman at Scalpay by the name of Campbell. He made good use of the natural harbour in that island and its strategic position nestling into East Loch Tarbert. It was both an anchorage and a landing place and could be gained on nights when the master of a larger vessel would not contemplate continuing up the sea loch to Tarbert. But Campbell's fortunes suffered, like those of many in the Highlands and Islands, when he gave shelter to the fleeing prince after the 1745 rebellion. The destruction of the clans which had supported the rebel cause did not end at Culloden. Even in the dangerous game of politics, Campbell of Scalpay was canny and somehow retained his lands.

So you could understand it if he was looking for a strategic match for his beautiful daughter, to rebuild the family fortunes. Like Clanranald to the south and so many others. But this story, which is also told between the lines of songs, does not go like that. He did have a daughter and she was known for her wit as well as her beauty. Like many women from a Scalpay background, she had jet-black hair and a dark complexion. They do say that the survivors of the Armada found shelter and new lives in that part of the world.

Anna Campbell had already met with the son of a well-known family of Stornoway shipowners and merchants – Morrisons. Their eldest son grew up with a love of the sea and his father had been wise enough not to fight it. The young man had mastered the sextant and his ship went to the Isle of Mann to trade. They say she would also continue to Ireland and across the Bay of Biscay to trade with Spanish ports.

Some would say that a marriage to a sailor was no life for a woman. She would be sharing her husband's deepest feelings with two other mistresses – his ship and the sea itself. Others said it was an ideal match for Anna, who was no ordinary woman. She would make use of the times when her husband was at sea. She composed songs and she even assisted her father in the running of his affairs. She was liked and respected by their tenants. It seemed that, on one island at least, times could be better again, after the suffering which devastated the Highlands and Islands after the insanity of the Jacobite march and the brutal reprisals.

So this was not the arranged match of other sad songs. Alan was a strong fellow, reddish-brown haired, and also well-liked by his crews. He could speak up for himself but did not waste words. So the understanding was there. It only needed the *reitach* to make the agreement public.

Some of the Morrisons would travel to Scalpay, by horse. Alan would, of course, take one of his father's vessels. There was no need of their great trading ship. So two seaworthy skiffs set off together from Stornoway to race for Scalpay. In the course of that passage you'll meet strong current close to the Shiant Islands. If you time it well you'll get help from the tide, which will sweep you on. If the wind turns against that tide, you could be in trouble in an open craft.

At Scalpay they grew anxious when they heard the wind howl. It was a full gale. They reassured each other that if any sailors would cope with that it was the Morrison boys. And it was a great relief to see a reefed-down lugsail at last enter the Kyles of Scarp. But there was only one. Anna rushed with the others to the north harbour and was there to hear what Alan's relations had to tell her.

They had met steep seas and overfalls. They were all struggling and the boats had separated. They lost sight of Alan's boat in a trough and they never saw her rise again. There was not a thing they could do, in these confused seas, but save their own craft.

Anna went out day after day, searching the shoreline. They say there was not a plank; nor tiller, nor keg, nor board from that missing vessel ever came ashore. And not one body was found on that grey, hard coastline. Many refused to believe that the great sailor and his brave crew were gone. But they say that Anna knew she would not be meeting her skipper in the world of harbours and commerce and cattle and weaving. She composed a song which is so painful it is nearly brutal. She had no will to continue living in a shore world which was without her brown-haired skipper. He did not even have a thin white shroud to keep him from the claws and teeth of the creatures of the sea.

Anna did not last long without him. It was as if all her energy had gone into that composition. Her burial was to have been at Rodel, by St Clement's Church. Campbell, her father, gave the task of taking her on her last voyage to her brother, also a handy sailor. Again, two boats departed a secure harbour and one of them had a small ship of oak secured on the boards. Again, they met with foul weather, when they were past the point of returning. Anna's brother had the heavier craft. She was known to be strong but she was struggling to rise with the building seas.

The skipper had to say that the living came before the dead. They cast the casket to the tides. They cast anchor and ballast and became more buoyant and made a landfall in one of the bays of Harris. They had come through it but the son had to tell his father he had lost the precious cargo.

The flood tide sets north-east, from out abeam East Loch Tarbert. That is the bearing of the Shiant Islands. Around the Shiants, the tidal forces are cyclical. So Alan Morrison had waited for his Anna Campbell in the waters close to these islands. That's likely where his skiff had been overpowered by breaking seas. And now Anna's body went on the flood tide towards the Shiants. She would retreat a bit on the ebb tide but the flood is stronger than the ebb in that area.

These are the forces that brought them at last together. Both of the bodies were washed up on the narrow neck of pebbles which joins two islands in that group. I can't say if they were buried together but I can say, first hand, that the area close to the Shiant Islands is abundant with life in the air and in the sea.

References

This is one of the best-known stories in Lewis, Harris and the Uists. I was first told it by Norman Malcolm MacDonald, author of the play *Anna Caimpbeul*. The Carmichael-Watson project describes Alexander Carmichael collecting several versions of the song including one from a Kate Urquhart of Taransay. There are many recordings of the song. An example from Flora MacNeil of Barra is at: http://folktrax-archive.org/menus/cassprogs/001scotsgaelic.htm. This was one of the songs used as a basis for the *confluence* project with Taigh Chearsabhagh, the arts centre in Lochmaddy, North Uist. A classic recording by the late Kitty MacLeod of Lewis ('generally regarded as the finest stylist among Gaelic folk-singers' – Alan Lomax) is used in the soundtrack of Andy MacKinnon's film. The same singer is also famous for composing the melody to go with another lyric of parted lovers, 'Calum Sgaire'.

Recorded traditions from Scalpay describe the vessel used by Anna's brother as 'the Canna boat' but there is another waulking song with that as a subject, so it is possible that two different stories, in two different songs, have become combined.

A CROSSING TO SCARP

Just in case you think that telling stories is a thing of the past, here's one I heard on the road from Scalloway to Lerwick, Shetland, in September 2013. But it took me back to the island of Scarp, off the west side of North Harris. After the last resident left in the 1960s, some of the abandoned houses were bought as holiday homes for a new seasonal community. I met a composer from Dusseldorf who set some of my poems to music and I crossed, several times, to join him at his house on Scarp. You can look down on the Sound from the cliff path which hugs the rock, northwards from the village of Hushinish.

The water is the most intense of blues and greens though it boils white in a strong wind. Some widely travelled seamen have told me that the seas to the north, when there is a deep Atlantic depression, are amongst the most steep they have ever seen. But on a fine day I can't think of a more spectacular landscape. There is a contrast between the bare rock of the high ridges, the white of the beaches and these sea colours. These days you are as likely to see the huge dark span of sea eagles as the wheeling golden eagles which also thrive in that territory.

But, as my mother, born in the village of Shawbost, Isle of Lewis, used to often say, 'You can't live on a view.' It's interesting to compare how Scalpay, with its natural harbour, survived as a community – now connected by bridge to the mainland – but Scarp could not hold its people.

Peter Campbell is a member of the trust which operates the restored gaff-rigged herring drifter from Lerwick called the Swan. *The Cape Farewell Project had just boarded the boat, to place artists and scientists together with a view to documenting how signs of climate change may be visible in the Shetland Islands. I happened to be in Shetland and went to a gathering aboard, to wish everyone well.*

Peter offered my wife and myself a lift back to our own small yacht, which was berthed in Lerwick. It's not a long drive but it seemed a very short one this night. This is how I remember his story.

'So you know Scarp?' he said. 'Well, you might not hear it in my voice, but I spent my early years there. My father was the schoolmaster. It was a great experience for my family, but the way of life was changing already. For instance, if a woman was expecting, they preferred her to make the crossing in good time and get ensconced in hospital, rather than risk an emergency.

'One woman had indeed crossed in good time so her baby was born with relatives on hand. She was driven back to Hushinish and the village boat was waiting there, to take her and her child back home. The baby was in a tiny carrycot in her man's care and she wrapped some blankets and a cover over it as there was a bit of a swell rolling in. After they'd pushed the boat out, they were committed. It would have been oars and the Seagull outboard motor, then – not so much power. As soon as they'd left, they were thinking that they maybe should have kept her where she was and found lodgings ashore for the new mother.

'But these fellows knew every inch of the way across, where to find the easier water, feeling their way down the Sound, timing it between the gusts. There was a huge rise and fall. On the tops of the waves they could see the shorelines and in the troughs the seas looked pretty much like the mountains behind them. And just as grey. But, to cut a long story short, the boat came through it with its particular cargo.

'You can be sure that mother was glad to get her carrycot ashore but surprised that there was no waiting arms to take it. The pier at Scarp was deserted. Usually there was no shortage of helpers. This night, when they were very much needed, there was none. One of the crew, a tall man, took the carrycot and set off towards her house while the rest of the crew secured their boat so she was safe. The husband of the new mother helped her to her home.

'When the mother, baby and the crewman reached the house, an island woman was standing at its gable. The mother and her husband had been expecting a warm welcome for bringing new life to Scarp but the lone woman sobbing by the gable was the only one to be seen.

'The new mother asked, "What on earth is wrong?" Her neighbour reacted by stretching out her hand to touch her and ask, "Is it you? Is it really yourself? Where have you come from?"

'The mother replied, "From the boat." But the other woman kept shaking her head. She simply could not believe what she was seeing.

'"Is it flesh and blood I'm seeing?"

'You see, the boat had disappeared from view in the first big swell and had not been sighted again from the Scarp shore. They thought she was gone. So they had all returned to their own houses, stricken with grief. The loss of the boat and her crew would have been the end of the island.

'Now I'd like to tell you that I remember all of that first-hand, myself, but I can't claim that. I've only heard it from some who were aboard that boat. You see, I was that baby in the carrycot.'

References

Thanks to Peter Campbell for permission to retell his family story and for checking over and correcting my memory of his account.

Donald J. MacLeod, *Memories of the Island of Scarp* (The Islands Book Trust, Isle of Lewis, 2011) is a lively memoir of the island. Angus Duncan (1888–1971) also published an excellent memoir, edited by his son (also A. Duncan) and including some superb retellings of ceilidh house tales: Angus Duncan, *Hebridean Island: Memories of Scarp* (Tuckwell Press, 1995, republished by Birlinn, Edinburgh, 2005). 'Big John, the King's Son' (p. 65) is an example of how a tale told all over Europe is developed into a recognisable local version by talented tellers. Angus Duncan's respect for his storytelling mentor is clear, as is the debt to travelling people who maintained a link with traditions in story and song after these connections had been lost amongst most folk. I have also heard a version of this story from Newfoundland, emphasising the boatbuilding part and suggesting that weakening traditions in Scotland were often continued in Gaelic-speaking parts of Canada, as highlighted in the published work of the folklorist Margaret Bennett.

I considered retelling the story of the king's three sons here but, the version in *Hebridean Island* seems to me so clear and measured that it is better to refer the reader to read it for themselves. It seems to me a strong example of how a person has lived with a story in its variants for so long that it has become a part of him.

6

LEWIS AND OUTLYING ISLANDS

WEST LEWIS

DALMORE

GALLAN HEAD

UIG

GT BERNERA

CALLANISH

LOCH ROAG

WEST NORTH LEWIS

MEALASTA

ISLE MEALASTA

SCARP

LOCH RESORT

AN ENDLESS VOYAGE

WEST LEWIS

Timber is in short supply all through the Outer Hebrides and it's difficult to make a roof without it. Some huge logs come ashore on the west sides of Lewis and Harris, maybe drifted all the way from Canada. It's possible they escaped the rafts of logs moved downstream for milling. Most of the driftwood seemed to pile up on the steep shores in the district of Uig, on mainland Lewis, and very little of it on Mealasta Island.

At last the men of Mealasta decided they could not trust to luck or charity any longer. So the lads prepared their best vessel, a real load-carrier, for the voyage south and through the Sound of Harris. Then they could bide their time at Rodel and look for a clear crossing to Gairloch. One of their number had a relation who ran an estate there. They could load their craft with a suitable stock of timbers for building their roofs.

The wives and mothers and sweethearts waved them off and tried not to show any anxiety. There had been swampings and drownings in the past and all parts of the planned voyage held their own challenges and dangers. They knew they would have to allow a period of time before they could expect to see the boat's return. These women were used to having to cope on their own when their men were taking their lambs or their dried cod and ling to market. But time passed slowly while the young men were gone. The days became weeks.

Enquiries were made and the Mealasta folk did indeed receive word that their men had made a good crossing and departed from the anchorage at Badachro, on the mainland, with their cargo as planned. There had been strong winds after they sailed so the suggestion was that they might have had to make landfall on the east side of Lewis or even at Scalpay. But there was no further word of them.

Now the womenfolk and the children and the whole island community were close to despair. It was a mercy that there was no sign of wreckage sighted along the jagged coasts. They might have made the Shiant Islands or made a landfall in some place where there was not even a track. But the weather had improved and no word of that strong and seaworthy Mealasta boat was received. You can't hold a wake, far less a burial, for men who are missing. The women couldn't carry on with their own lives. The community lost strength and skill, as well as the loved individual quirks of the fathers and sons.

One woman had a promise from one of the missing lads. She missed his voice and the look of him and his hand in her own as they walked out, away from the village. She woke one night with his voice in her ears. He told her how they had weathered a gale on the North Minch and made landfall in a deep sea-loch, north of Scalpay. But they had not made the shore. Their cargo of timber had been sighted by those who could also find a use for it. The men, exhausted from their fight with the sea, could not defend themselves. They had been killed and hidden and their boat dismembered, so there would be no evidence.

She couldn't tell the others what she'd heard. So she gathered all the phrases into a song. That did not provide much comfort. But it did share her heartbreak. Some chose to continue to hope.

A year or more later, some of the Mealasta folk were persuaded to visit their relations close to the town of Stornoway. It was the time of the Bennadrove market. There would be gingerbread and lemonade in bottles, with glass marbles trapped in their neck as stoppers. There would be bidding and tunes and a distraction for the women. Most of their friends and relations thought they had already grieved too long, with no bodies to bury.

The young woman who had composed the song of her dream went with the others. They joined the line of cheery people at the gingerbread stall. She stopped in her own footsteps, rooted to the trodden ground. She stared at the back and shoulder of a fisherman's gansey, in front of her. The patterns show the village of the seaman and every single one has something that's a little different from any other. She recognised that one because she had knitted it herself, for the man she loved. Her heart beat hard against her own ribs but when the man turned it was a stranger. She knew then that she had heard the truth from the lad, come to her in the night.

I can't say if that gansey was evidence enough for the ways of the law but I have no doubt that a justice of a sort was done. I don't know how much that would have eased the pain of the people of Mealasta.

But I did hear that the women of that island took charge of the smaller vessel, left on the beach. They had all taken their place in the boats from a young age and now they took guidance from one of the old men, no longer strong enough to go to sea himself. They say that the women's handling of the boat was much admired in the districts of Uig and on the neighbouring island of Scarp.

References
Version in Donald MacDonald, *Tales and Traditions of The Lews* (Birlinn, Edinburgh, 2009). Additional elements are from the telling of Maggie Smith, heard at the Tip of the Tongue Festival, Isle of Jura, 2012. The Gaelic song with the dream of the girl whose fiancée discloses their fate is translated by Donald S. Murray and quoted by Bill Lawson.

WHO WAS CHASING WHO?

Every culture, rural or urban, has its bogeyman stories. On the Island of Lewis the figure was known as Mac an t-Sronaich. Sometimes this is translated as 'son of the long-nosed one', but most people seem to think there was a real live person, who hailed from the district of Sronaich, on the mainland. There is some evidence that there was a vagrant or nuisance but little evidence that this man really did commit murder. That did not stop my uncle Kenny Murdo Smith from telling tale after tale, which I now know came from his own father. As children, we loved to be scared when our uncle was babysitting.

The way I remember his stories, people, especially bright youngsters, quite often got the better of the outlaw. Every district seems to have its own cave linked to the fugitive. If he used every one of them, he got around even more than Bonnie Prince Charlie, who also has many points and cairns with his name on them.

In Stornoway they say that Mac an t-Sronaich was given some shelter and food at the window of a manse across the moor, in Keose. The minister's wife was related in some way.

Some stories are still surfacing and my favourite is very much in sympathy with the tone of those told me by my uncle.

Mac an t-Sronaich ranged wide and far over the moors and took what he wanted to keep himself alive. It seems he reached as far as the district of Uig and further, over the hills till you were close to the remote communities at Tamnavay and at the head of Loch Resort. They say that two men set off to join the cliff path by Scarp, to buy a piggy of whisky for a *reitach* or a wedding. When they failed to return, it was found that they had paid their money and taken the jar but neither of them were seen again.

That was the sort of deed folk said must have been the work of Mac an t-Sronaich, but I could think of a few other possible explanations for the disappearance of these men. Not so far from that terrain, another chase took place.

The herring would come in to Loch Tamnavay in season. It was thick with them and good hauls could be made. But one village lost their herring net to an army of dogfish that left it in tatters. At other times that would have been another blessing, for the oil from the liver of that species was valuable. But it was a curse when the herring were at their prime. They were full fish, at the height of the summer.

So one fit fisher-lad, by the name of Dohmnall Ruadh Beag, set off to cover the miles over the moor to bring back a replacement. It was heavy and sweaty work, with all these yards of treated cotton, in a parcel, draped around his shoulders.

The ties broke and he just gathered the whole dark thing, dangling corks and all, about his chest. He was barefoot of course, so he just rolled his breeks up to his thighs and enjoyed the relief of the cool damp peaty ground on his warm feet and ankles.

What he didn't know was that Mac an t-Sronaich was stalking him, looking to come in and steal what he could, when his man weakened. He drew in closer when Dohmnall Ruadh Beag was about to descend at *Beinn a Deas*. But when he crept over a mound he saw a strange creature, like a giant insect, with a dark web around its broad shoulders and white spindly legs under that.

He took to his heels at once. Mac an t-Sronaich was known to be a fierce wiry man who could fight anything human, but this had to be a creature from another terrible world. He thought the hardy wee redhead was the devil himself.

References
Based on Maggie Smith's recording of Finlay MacIver: http://www.hebrideanconnections.com/Details.aspx?subjectid=8596. See also the same informant's description of curing haddock:

> It wasn't left in the salt for very long at all. They used to say that if you took the eyes out of the haddock, as much salt as the two hollows would hold, that that was enough to salt the fish. Too much salt and it was far too salty. Then they hung it above the fire. In the winter it was half smoked and it kept them in meals until the spring. It was soaked first of all to remove part of the salt.

A FATHER AND A SON

The feuds of the past often began as disputes over livestock. More often than not, the cattle and sheep of different clans would graze together, outwith fences. When they were gathered, each owner would identify their animals from a system of small cuts made in the ears. To this day, the earmarks of sheep on Lewis, village to village, are like an alternative language of their own.

The MacLeods of Pabbay kept some of their stock on that island, off the fertile Valtos peninsula which juts out into West Loch Roag, in the south-west of Lewis. But they also allowed some of their beasts to roam and graze on the rich strips of grass between the sandy shore on the mainland and the higher ground. That was the territory of the MacAulays, another powerful clan at that time. Old Norman MacLeod, of Pabbay, was a brother of the MacLeod clan chief, so he also carried some weight.

Once, old Norman was looking on as his herdsman drove a beast or two on to the beamy vessel they used, to take stock to and from the island. A heavy bull would sometimes be towed along to swim behind, on a calm day. But this time the herdsman of the MacAulays was also at the shore. He saw that one of their own animals was being herded in, along with the MacLeod stock.

First he was polite, asking to see the earmarks, just to make sure. But neither old Norman's hearing nor his eyesight were of the best any longer. He grew defensive and then aggressive. The MacAulay herdsman had a hand on one horn and old Norman MacLeod had his hand on the other. The MacAulay man gave a pull and Norman tipped over into the hull. He came up with his mouth full of blood, howling in pain.

By the time he got across to his home, he had calmed down and probably realised he'd been in the wrong. It had cost him two of his teeth. He took to his bed with a dram to ease the pain. But his wife was very strong-willed too. Their five sons returned from the Flannan Isles, some 20 miles out from Loch Roag. They kept sheep out there. The lads' mother threw the two teeth on the table and said that the insult had to be revenged. The family could not be known as cattle-thieves.

The strong young men took their longswords and their daggers and crossed to the mainland while their father still slept. They divided themselves in the dark. There was just enough moon, through the cloud, to make out the form of the MacAulay houses, built into the hard ground, back from the shore. Each house was struck, with the benefit of surprise. They sought only the young, able-bodied men of the clan. These young men were killed as they woke. None of them, nor their mothers nor wives nor their children, would have known of any reason for the brutal attack. When the light came up, the extent of the massacre was known. There was not one able-bodied young man of that extended family left alive, in Valtos.

But the brothers had not managed to slay every single MacAulay who could avenge their act. There was one of that family who had been taken away from Valtos, an orphan fostered out to a childless couple at Mealasta, further down the coast.

Norman MacLeod was horrified when he came to discover the murders his sons had committed. He met at once with his brother the chief, fearing an endless feud that would claim more and more lives, in time.

They agreed that the murderous sons had forfeited their rights to the land and its stock. But the chief suggested one thing more. The MacAulay lad who was fostered out to these poor people should be given a proper education. This would be a sign that the elder clan members were not implicated in the deed. The young John Roy MacAulay was to be taken into their own family and treated with all respect. That was the only thing which could break the circle.

Thus the surviving young man of the Valtos MacAulays was taken into Norman MacLeod's home on Pabbay while his elder sons had to make their own way in the world. His foster-father at Mealasta, a man known as Dark Finlay, was heartbroken at the parting but he knew that he could not offer the same advantages.

Old Norman doted on the growing lad. The waters around Pabbay Mor abound with the best of fish, turbot and haddock and sweet dabs. Sea-trout run through the sound, migrating towards the fresh water where a red burn enters the next bay. John Roy was taught to set a line and cast one too. He was taken to the hill, as soon as his legs were strong enough, to discover how you could steal upwind close enough to a herd of deer to have a chance of taking one.

Norman's wife did not take to the lad, who seemed to her to be taking the place of their own sons. The lads themselves, when they did visit the family home, took every chance to mock the youngster or trip him up in some way. At the same time, Dark Finlay would lie awake, wondering how his foster-son was faring at the hands of the MacLeods.

Norman did his best. He told his sons that the only way they could make any amends for their hasty action was to show kindness to young John Roy. He urged them to take the lad along, next time they went to take a deer. He was already strong enough to run with them and could manage a horse or a dog with the best of them. He also had a keen eye and could already hit his mark with an arrow.

The MacLeods would take to the high ground, up from Mealasta, in the quest for fresh venison. The deer-ground extended as far as the deep inlet of Loch Resort. Not far beyond that, at the shoulder of a rise, they maintained a simple hut – an *airigh* or bothy. This was where they stayed when they drove animals to their summer pasture. And this is where they found shelter when they hunted deer in the winter.

At last the five MacLeod sons agreed to take John Roy along with them, look after him well and take him in to the comradeship of the hunt. The youth knew nothing of the history and was happy to be initiated, a coming of age. Norman had them swear to look after him well and not place him at risk.

They left with excited dogs and plenty of provisions. They took a route very close to John Roy's earlier home at Mealasta. Then they took to the hill, with the youngest running ahead, not knowing to conserve his energy. He'd learn soon enough.

The day was bright but the wind was chill, promising a flurry of snow. The next day it did fall but old Norman had known the warm shelter of a good going peat fire in that *airigh* often enough in his own youth. He was not too anxious.

It was Dark Finlay who woke in the night, at his simple house at Mealasta. He looked out to see the snowfall. His wife urged him to return to the warmth. Finlay had stirred with the images of a dream.

He could see the son he'd fostered, in danger. His wife urged him to try to sleep. Again he started up, seeing John Roy, exposed and shivering. The third time he woke, he had the sight of that *airigh*, beyond Loch Resort, and could see the youth bound up outside. He lost no more time.

Finlay found warm clothing and went to the byre to fill a vessel with milk, warm from the cow. He covered that and wrapped it in skins to keep it warm. Then he was off, still a fit man for his age. But when he came to the snow-coated track, where his prints would be left for any to find, he began to walk backwards. So he left a trail which would suggest that a man had come from the slope beyond Loch Resort, northwards, over the hill. It could be followed only to the coastal slopes and there it would fade.

Dark Finlay strode on, still an immensely strong man for his age. He could stride the hill backwards faster than most could go forwards. At last he came close to the site of the bothy. It was there he heard a faint cry. He found the pitiful scene he had already glimpsed three times. John Roy had been taken out and bound to a rock, with hardly a stitch on him to save him from the cold. He was at the very last of his endurance. No doubt the five brothers planned to return with some story of the young lad being separated from themselves in a blizzard.

Soon he was huddled in skins and a plaid of wool. The warm milk was put to his lips and he began to revive. Then the foster-father let his son fall over a shoulder. Now he walked forwards, retracing the steps he'd already made in the snow. He knew well that these murderous young men would stop at nothing. It would seem as if John Roy had revived and found the path by himself. But there would be no clue as to where he had gone, once the tracks faded, at the lower ground.

Finlay took his precious burden inland, to a cave that gave them shelter for a time. He put the care of John Roy to a man he could trust and sought out Norman MacLeod. The old man was heartbroken at the actions of his own sons. They were cast out from MacLeod lands there and then, but both men knew that John Roy would not be safe, on Lewis, for some years to come. Together, they arranged for him to be taken by sea to relations on the island of Mull, once he was fully recovered.

He would receive the best of education there. He would learn to speak other languages and to write and recite. But he would also take his uncanny skills with the bow even further and learn how to handle both the long blade and the short.

John Roy did flourish on Mull. He did return to Lewis in time and meet with Finlay and his wife, who had protected him and saved him. He did meet again with the five brothers who had left him for dead. But that really is another story and we'd best leave it there, where the dreams of the foster-father saved the life of his adopted son.

References
Based on a short but clear synopsis, told to me by Maggie Smith round my kitchen table in Stornoway, November 2013. Her version is based on her recording of John M. MacLeod, former headmaster of Balallan school, sadly passed away in January 2014. Maggie generously shared this research with me and some elements are included.

The same story is told in a very detailed form as the very first tale in the Morrison manuscript. It leads on to an epic tale of revenge. It may be that the oral tale has continued to exist, passed by word of mouth in different areas of Lewis. But it is also possible that Morrison's transcription of the story, placed by him as starting in August 1460 with the murder committed by Norman MacLeod's sons, has preserved the details which may well have been otherwise lost.

The Tale of the Head of the Flounder

We used to wait for the second tug before hauling up a line. You wanted a 'double-header' – haddock or whiting on each of the two hooks. These were suspended on a wire thing like a coat-hanger but with a lump of lead in the middle. At first the two species looked alike and you couldn't tell by size, then. We would usually take home haddock and whiting of two to three pounds in weight. Then one of the old fellows – that would be a man of more than 50 – he'd point out the thumb-mark. The whiting only had a tiny black speckle at the pectoral fin but the haddock (or haddie, as we called them) had the mark of Peter's thumb. I was told it happened at the feeding of the five thousand.

Last night I ate one of the tastiest and firmest fleshed fish of the sea – a John Dory. In Gaelic that's *iasg-Pheadair* (Peter's fish) and that species also carries the thumb-mark. I've heard both haddock and John Dory called 'the tribute fish'. I knew many names of fish in Gaelic as well as English because different words were used for subtle distinctions, perhaps like grading according to size.

Saithe and lythe, or pollack and coalfish, had the most names between the two species. They looked alike to me at first and we caught them on the same rocky territory. Again, the difference was quietly pointed out. The lower lip of the lythe sticks out as if the fish was sulking. And that brings us to the flounder.

Some fish are called kingfish or king's fish or are said to be the property of the queen, but once there was a proper gathering to decide, once and for all, which fish deserved to be the king of all fish.

Naturally, Poseidon decided to hold the contest in the North Minch. That was when the grounds were still abundant.

So they came from near and far. The bright red gurnards walked along the bottom on their spiky pectorals. Other species swam, in their different layers of sea, from the deeps to the surface. It was an immense gathering of the abundant and varied species to be found around our islands. That fellow MacGillivray, the one who walked from Harris to Aberdeen to study the natural kingdom and then returned to paint the John Dory, the dragonet and the gurnard along with many others – he would have had a field day if he'd seen it.

You might be surprised to hear who was chosen. It was not the powerful conger or the fast mackerel. If you've ever seen one caught with a bare hook in its delicate mouth, you wouldn't be surprised. This is the one, described by another Lewisman thus:

> … when alive has a beautiful sheen, alternating from crimson to purple shades which disappear when dead. When newly taken from the water it utters a pensive, faint cry resembling that of a mouse.

The same fellow describes how they spawn and how they shoal and adds:

> Unlike other fish they swim against the wind. *

Aye, that's the herring. They were chosen partly for their beauty and partly for their usefulness to us folk who walk on land. But they were also chosen for their way of life. Unlike the mackerel or most other species, they do not eat up their own young. Instead they glide through the water and suck in the glints of plankton. That's why a shiny bare hook at dusk is the best way to catch them.

Most of the other fish, slight and great, in the assembly could see the point. They just shrugged their fins and flicked their tales and returned to their feeding or their migration. But there was a latecomer to the proceedings. A flounder, hugging the contours of the bottom, arrived only when the stragglers were shoaling together for a last yarn – the way we do on Lewis, even our fish.

The flounder really thought she was in with a very good chance. 'How did it all go then?' she asked a passing *bodach ruadh* (reddish cod that lives amongst the kelp).

When she was told that the herring was now officially the king of the fish she did not take it too well. 'So I suppose that's that then. Where does that leave me?' she said but she twisted up her mouth as she said it.

Poseidon must have noticed that she was such a poor loser because the flounder's mouth stayed that way. In fact her descendants still have that curious twist in the mouth, to this very day.

References
* quoted from Norman Morrison, *My Story* (Inverness, 1937).

A version of this tale is told in Dalmore, Lewis, according to D.J. MacLennan, *Dalmore: Tales of a Lewis Village* (http://5dalmore.blogspot.co.uk/). See also Kenneth MacDonald, *Peat Fire Memories: Life in Lewis in the Early Twentieth Century* (Tuckwell Press, East Linton, 2003), from his memory of stories told at a ceilidh house in Sandwick, Lewis. There is a similar tradition recorded by

Alexander Carmichael, *Carmina Gadelica* (Scottish Academic Press, Edinburgh, 1971, vol. VI, p. 96), and still told in Ireland. The flounder gives a very cheeky retort to Colum Cille after he treads on her and he responds by telling her that the sneering twist in her mouth would stay with the species forever. Strangely enough, a version very similar to the North Lewis one was published in *The Western Mail* (Perth, Australia, Thursday, 15 January 1951).

A Transaction

There are many variations of the encounters of more naïve village folk with the ways of the town. Another uncle of mine, Calum 'Safety' Smith, recreates the move of a large family from the village of Shawbost to the outskirts of Stornoway in his memoir Around the Peat-Fire. *He describes the period between the two world wars but he also retells this village tale, which he suggests may be from the nineteenth century. The story may well have been lost, like many told by Calum's father, Murdo Finlay, if a son had not taken the initiative to transfer it from the spoken to the written. Like all the other tales in this book, it is now retold again, rather than reproduced in the recorded wording.*

When times were hard, as they usually were, village folk would walk considerable distances, across the moor to the town, with any produce they thought they might be able to sell. One woman learned how to distil a potent whisky from a little spare grain. She asked around her neighbours and, sure enough, one of them also distilled the illegal spirit and told her of an address in town she should take it to.

So she set off with her best produce in two corked clay jars. It's over 18 miles from Shawbost to Stornoway by the road. It's still a long distance if you take the shorter route, the saddle between the hills, walking barefoot on moorland.

At last she came out on the old Pentland Road. She took her boots from her pack then and put them on to follow the road into the town. She asked for the street name she'd been given. She was taken in and whispered her business to the man of the house.

'It was no friend of yours that gave you this address,' he said. 'This is the house of the exciseman.'

She realised then that her neighbour didn't want any competition in her trade. But the fellow could see at a glance that she needed every penny to keep her family so he whispered another address she might try.

She made her deal there and the precious liquid was decanted into other containers, once the buyer had tasted a sample.

On her way back, she crossed a burn. Of course she was thirsty after all that walking. So she rinsed out one of the jars and filled it with cold water. She drank deeply and walked on. But they say she was far from straight in her walking when she appeared again in her home village.

So it must have been a very powerful spirit produced at home, in the stills of Shawbost.

References
Retold from Calum Smith, *Around the Peat-Fire* (Birlinn, Edinburgh, 2001, reprinted 2004).

THE BLIND WOMAN OF BARVAS

As you proceed north up the west side of the Island of Lewis, sheltered inlets become more and more scarce. Cliffs fall away to the ocean
and surf beaches, with treacherous cross currents, stretch out between
them. Once you clear Loch Roag, there are very few sheltered places till
you round the Butt of Lewis, at the very north of the Lewis mainland.

The shore at Barvas is one of the most exposed. In the past, folk had
little alternative but to risk launching the village boat into the pounding seas. But the risks were so high here that the Barvas boat never put
to sea until the word came from the adjacent villages, north and south,
that the fish were running. Most fishermen thought dogfish were a
curse, bursting the herring nets. But the Barvas folk were known as
the *biorach* after the name of the piked dogfish they sought. When
skinned, the firm flesh holds together well. It is good eaten fresh, but it
also takes the salt. So they valued this species as winter fare. You would
see lines of them drying in the wind. Then they would keep for some
months.

The word came from Bragar, to the south, that the *biorach*
were indeed running. It seemed a decent day so the Barvas boat

was launched. Everyone would lend a hand or a shoulder to get her down on smooth boards. Then the round ballast stones would be passed out so she would be as stable as she could be.

But, this day, the lads were caught out in a sudden gale. Night fell and she had not yet returned. The shore was lined with all the able-bodied folk in the village. They were showing lanterns, hoping that they could guide their loved ones back to the home shore.

The skipper's mother happened to be a blind woman. She had lost her sight before her firstborn arrived. Now she was listening, while the rest were watching for a scrap of brown cloth visible above the turbulent white.

There is one word, in Gaelic, for the sound of pebbles running back down a sloping shore after a wave. She heard that all right but some-thing else as well. She knew it was the disturbance caused by a body, cast up from the sea. The shock brought her sight back.

So she saw that son for the first time when his body was returned to the shore at Barvas, after the boat was swamped.

References

Told to me during a coastguard watch at the Stornoway station by my then colleague, John D. Smith, from Barvas. John is a 'Lewis cousin' – that is, not a first one and maybe not even a second. He features as 'The Barvas Navigator' in the writing of Hector MacDonald, or Aimsir Eachainn, first published in the West Highland Free Press, then collected in two volumes as *Views from North Lochs* and *More Views from North Lochs* (Birlinn, Edinburgh, 2007, 2009).

I did not take notes at the time but John has such a presence as a storyteller that the story has always stayed with me. He introduced it as a village tradition but I have not so far encountered another recorded version.

EAST LEWIS

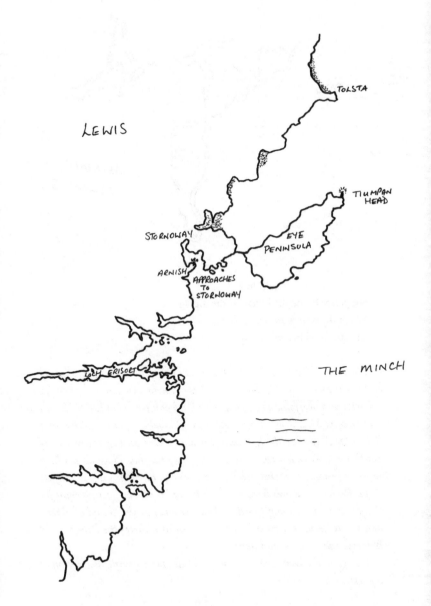

LEWIS

TOLSTA

TIUMPAN HEAD

STORNOWAY

EYE PENINSULA

ARNISH

APPROACHES TO STORNOWAY

LOCH ERISORT

THE MINCH

THE BLUE MEN OF THE STREAM

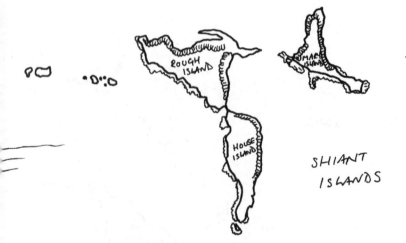

When your bow is colliding
but you're losing the breeze in the dip.
When the waters are standing
and the flood breaks through at a rip.

The Sound of Shiants is the stretch of water between the rocky coastline of east Lewis and an archipelago which lies out across an area infamous for tide-rips and overfalls. The Lewis mainland points of Gob Rubh' Uisenis and Gob na Milaid mark the southern and northern points, with minor lights. Don't confuse the first with the major Usinish Light, east side of South Uist. We've left that point a long way behind. Place names keep recurring throughout the Hebrides so you've to be careful not to confuse them. Remember there's Berneray with Barra Head, our starting point for this route north, through stories, then Berneray in the Sound of Harris and Great Bernera, west side of Lewis. And then there's the Pabbays and Borerays and Scalpays and Ronas.

    Let's go to the West Coast of Scotland Pilot for a specific description of the territory:

These islands are not permanently inhabited but afford pasture to a number of sheep and home to a profusion of seabirds. Eilean an Tighe, the S part of the largest island in the group, has precipitous cliffs on its E side and is lower than Garbh Eilean, the N part, to which it is joined by Mol Mor, a distinctive, low, narrow and stony isthmus.

This is an excellent description of the territory of the blue men, or at least what you can see of it from the surface. Some people say they are descended from the ghosts of sad Moorish people, taken by the Vikings in the ninth century and lost at sea, on their route north. Others say they are, like selkies, the souls of dead mariners. They might have been caught in the overfalls which occur here when strong wind works against spring tides. People say different things but most are agreed as to the appearance and behaviour of the blue men.

They take a hold of your vessel. You might see a long thin hand appear over the gunnel or you might sense them holding you back. Your craft could be caught there forever, at the mercy of rising wind, but the blue men give you a chance.

In our part of the world it's usually eloquence which can save you or at least a sharp wit. The challenges of the blue men are, of course, cried out in Gaelic. One after another, from the lowest to the chief, each will pose a riddle or offer a line of verse. One after another, from the ship's boy to the skipper, the crew must respond, matching rhythm as well as wit.

Once, a beamy open skiff was trying to work through the Sound and on to Loch Erisort. She was gripped by the arms of the blue men. The skipper hushed his lads. He knew to wait for the questions which were the nearest thing to a lifeline that they could hope to get.

The first one came, a whine above the cold wind. 'How many cables would you need, to reach from the keel of your ship to the bottom under you now?'

The crew were not allowed to talk it over and they did not have much time to respond. All looked to the young lad, his first trip aboard.

'One,' he said. 'One, if it was long enough.'

Their captors conceded that one. The next one came.

'And what's the sharpest thing in all the worlds?'

The man at the halyard took that challenge. 'The sharpest thing in the world I know, and maybe in your one too, is hunger.'

There was a gasp, which the crew took to mean they had come through that one, too. But the chief himself put his thin head above the surface now. He smiled in the knowledge that their next question should win them this small catch.

'What am I thinking?'

I think you can guess the answer to that one, from a story you've heard already: 'You're thinking you're talking to the skipper but you've only just reached me, the mate. And we've matched you on every point so far.'

The skipper didn't get off that easily, though. The chief of the blue men was not yet willing to release his own grip on the oak keel. 'You'd better put forward the man in command,' he said.

The skipper looked over the gunnel. He did not look that impressive. He was nearly bald and had a ruddy face. The skipper of a Lewis boat is chosen by the rest of the crew. There's no shortage of good seamen but the skipper has to be able to think on his feet. He looked for the eyes of the elusive shape he saw in the water. He did not find them but he heard the whine of the chief's voice, above the wind.

The chief of the blue men gave out his own volley:

The loudest noise you'll ever hear.
The swiftest thing in all the worlds
The tightest course you'll ever steer?

The Lewis skipper thought for a minute and then gave out his best reply.

After the sheets of light appear
the hammer of Thor will part the skies
and tear the skin of the drum of your ear.

There was a sigh of relief from the crew. Their vessel was giving a good account of itself. The skipper was encouraged to continue and confident enough to vary the rhythm:

Fire is a very swift thing
but the north wind itself
is that bit more keen.

Every man and boy on the skiff knew the answer to the last one. The skipper spoke for them all:

If the course can't vary one degree
that will take more than a hand that's true
that will require honesty.

His mate spoke up then, out to the elusive blue men. 'And if you know anything of honesty, you and your clan will release us now.'

They were free. It's a huge relief when the tide slacks off against the wind. Some turbulence remains but gradually the waters fall and the plunging diminishes. Soon the wind is driving you forward and the tide is assisting. There's a long wake through the water behind you and the transits are shifting all the time.

References
I've grown up with so many versions of the myth of the blue men that it's impossible for me to list all the sources. There is a short synopsis of the tale of the blue men in George Douglas (1856–1935), *Scottish Fairy and Folk Tales* (A.L. Burt, New York, 1901). But I do not know of any recorded or published account of the actual dialogue which takes place, apart from a brief contemporary version in English by Fitzroy MacLean (Collins, 1985 and Canongate, Edinburgh, 1990).

It may well be a challenge for the storyteller to invent some spontaneous lines of verse or heightened language. But there are many recordings of stories which use the pattern of the three questions. Often these are part of a retelling of a well-known type of international tale such as 'The Wise Peasant Girl'. Thus I've taken the liberty of splicing in variations of the types of question and answer told in the riddles associated with the now mythical historical figure of George Buchanan. Similar rhyming riddles occur in the ballads collected by James Francis Child (1882–98).

For Scottish variants on The Three Questions see Bruford and MacDonald 30a, b and c. See also several recordings relating to George Buchanan, held at the School of Scottish Studies. Other versions have been recorded from Angus MacLellan, some transcribed and translated by John Lorne Campbell.

It is interesting to compare this legend with the tradition of the MacVurichs, the bards from the Uists. If the crew are sufficiently eloquent they can conjure up the wind they want.

THE SPOONS OF HORN

As you come close to the town of Stornoway on the main road which comes north from Harris, a small road branches off eastwards towards the village of Grimshader. This frames a section of bogland known as Arnish Moor. There are trout lochs and, to seaward, a cairn which commemorates Prince Charlie's flight down the Minch. When I was young, I'd fish these lochs and I'd follow the burns in the hope of a sea-trout which had found its way up. But we never camped out. There were always stories of a haunting. A figure was said to appear not far from the crossroads.

One story told of a fellow on a small motorbike seeing the figure of a desperate boy running along beside the road, trying to stop him. But there were much older stories linked to that place.

My mother's brother, Kenny Murdo, was married to a woman from the village of Grimshader and I used to help out at the village fanks, or sheep-gatherings. I'd also help cut peats and be rewarded with huge feasts of filled rolls and fresh baking, before we went to the lochs or cast for red codling

in the sea-loch. There were always stories and not long ago I met with the
nephew of one of the Grimshader neighbours. As a Gaelic speaker who'd
grown up in the village, he could remember more than I did.

He remembered my uncle and his grandfather swapping yarns. There
were many sightings, over the years, of strange things on the moorland
between the village and the road to town. And there was some evidence of
an incident which happened back in the 1700s.

It's nothing new for lads to skip a day off school, to find better things
to do. These two fellows went out the Arnish moor in a hunt for birds'
eggs. I don't know if that was gulls' eggs or the eggs of grouse for eating
or, more likely, the rare eggs people stole and pierced and blew, to
make dry shells for collectors.

There was a dispute. Maybe one lad made a valuable find first and
didn't want to share it. But it came to blows. In the heat of the fight,
one of them put his hand on a loose rock and swung it at the other's
head and that was that.

The one who was left standing rooted around and found the
bleached bones of an animal, a sheep or a deer. He dug with those and
covered up the body of his friend.

At that time there were Baltic traders in and out of Stornoway every
day, carrying herrings and kippers. Often they were a man short when
they sailed and sometimes they'd take on an apprentice, on the spot, if
a fellow was free to travel.

I suppose this boy told the captain he was an orphan. His clothing
showed he was poor enough. The lad served his time and moved from
ship to ship and saw much of the world as the years passed. But most
people have a longing to see the place they grew up in, even if they've
lost touch with their people or there's a reason not to go back.

Eventually he was on a ship which was putting in to Stornoway.
He could have jumped ship in the last port but somehow he had not
been able to do that. So there they were, seeing the white beacon at
the tip of brown Arnish Point. Across the bay were the green banks of
Stoneyfield farm. There was a dense smoke over the stone houses back
from the three piers. You could smell the coal and you could smell
the oak dust from the kippering sheds. They glided past the boatyard

at Goat Island and the scent of hot pitch joined all the other senses that make up the combined smells of your home town. That had not changed much.

Of course he never told his shipmates he had family here and of course he could not be seen to be lurking aboard when there was a lively harbourside. He was sure no harm could come from visiting the Star Inn, right on the street they call South Beach. He took his pint of ale there and asked for some of the hot food from the pot of stew simmering on the range. Fresh mutton was a welcome change from salt pork.

It was served in a bowl of bound slats of wood, with a horn spoon to sup it. He put his hand on the spoon but he could not put it to the bowl. He could not move at all. His eyes were out the open door, looking directly across the bay to the Arnish Moor. He remembered the very route he'd taken that time he'd skived school with the boy who was then his friend. But it was the spoon that did it. He had looked through the pockets of the boy he'd killed with a stone, before digging a place for him in the moor. He had no thought of robbing him. He was maybe looking in case there was something he carried that would definitely identify the bones, if they were ever found.

There was nothing much but the horn spoon that most lads carried. It was the double of the one he now held in his hand. He'd returned the other to the pocket of the corpse and laid it under the turfs he'd cut. But now he stared at the spoon in his own hand as if there was blood on it.

Maybe it was his strange behaviour that drew attention to him. A few folk gathered to ask if he was all right and then, of course, someone or other thought he looked a bit familiar. 'Who are your people?'

His voice still showed he was local. You can't hide a Stornoway twang for long. And at last someone guessed he was one of the two boys who had disappeared at the same time, all these years ago.

The story is that he confessed and met his end on Gallows Hill, looking right over the town. Of course there are others who will tell you that the spoon he held was made not from horn but from a pile of the bones of deer or sheep, picked up near the peat-cuttings, out on Arnish Moor. Only this spoon was not made from animal bone. And it was not his imagination that blood appeared on bone.

The details within this story change from version to version, both oral and written, but there is some recent evidence of a more scientific nature. Human remains were found, during peat-cutting, near the place where the Grimshader road branches off. That is the area where so many sightings had been reported. It was no primitive form of man and there was not even any evidence of the ligature often found with bog-bodies as a sign of a ritual killing.

These remains were dated as seventeenth century. It was the body of a young male. The cause of death was a devastating blow to the back of the head delivered by a right-handed person. He was poorly dressed but the fabric of his clothing was still intact, including a bandage-type repair to his woollen stocking. He carried little in his pockets but a horn spoon.

References

I am indebted to the late Bill 'Taibhse' (Ghosty) MacDonald and Kenny Murdo Smith, Grimshader and Stornoway for this story. Also a conversation with Bill's grandson, Donnie 'Duvall' MacDonald. My own storytelling, like young Donnie's, is very much indebted to Audy MacIver, who returned to Lewis to live in Grimshader and became very much one of that group.

I gratefully acknowledge the work and the conversations of the late Frank Thompson, of Stornoway, a man steeped in local history and traditions and author of many non-fiction publications (also author of poems and short stories). See Francis Thompson, *The Supernatural Highlands* (Robert Hale and Co., London, 1976; republished by Luath, Edinburgh, 1997).

See also details of the body uncovered in the peat on Arnish Moor: http://canmore.rcahms.gov.uk/en/site/318142/details.

The Tooth of the Fairy Dog

When you mention Holm Point, most people think of the reefs known as the Beasts of Holm, extending out from there and marked by a green spar. That was where the motor yacht Iolaire *struck on New Year's Night 1919. Much has been written of that tragedy, most recently,* When I Heard the Bell: The Loss of the Iolaire, *by John MacLeod.*

*Norman Malcolm MacDonald's writing on the subject includes a well-researched factual account and an imaginative response in fiction. There is a small bilingual volume published by Acair, Stornoway (*Call na h-Iolaire*) and a spare but strong poem in his slim collection* Fàd. *But there is also a powerful chapter in his novel,* Portrona. *The historical event is well documented but the extent of the tragedy is so huge that it is still difficult to take in. This is more than a story and beyond the scope of this book. I refer the reader to the titles listed in the notes to this chapter.*

There are other layers of stories, factual and fanciful, linked to the fertile Holm peninsula. It extends to the village of Sandwick, up from conglomerate rock at Holm Point, capped with green turfs. The Coastguard lookout is no longer there, nor the aerial, nor the post from which we showed the black cone for a gale warning.

Holm has had a reputation as a place linked to the supernatural for countless years. Naturally, the old-time Coastguards would wind up the green volunteers, especially the young women, with their ghost stories on the middle watch. But one night I saw, with my own eyes, a substantial

*green-enamelled MF radio transceiver move by itself across the desk. The
senior watch officer looked at me and I looked at him.*

'You'd better go out and find out what's going on,' he said.

*A cow's foot had got tangled up in the cable outside, where it was not
very well secured, before going through the ducting into the shed.*

*Now and again people would call in for a cup of tea to help you pass the
time in a quiet watch and I now realise it was one of the best storytelling
environments I've ever known. The district of Holm was famous for tales
of people who had a special knowledge. Unusually these were linked to a
male figure rather than a female. Kenneth MacDonald tells one family
story which explains exactly how his great-great grandfather received his
special powers.*

There was one place along the green-topped cliffs where the grass
burned with an even more intense colour than the rest of it, in contrast
to the dull, pebbled stone. The story goes that a man by the name
of Alasdair, from a few generations back, was making his way by the
usual coastal route, to Holm Point, a good fishing place. It was a fine
mild night, but, even in these fairly bright conditions, he saw the grass
shine. He sensed the form of a man. He could hardly make out his
features but he could hear his voice clearly.

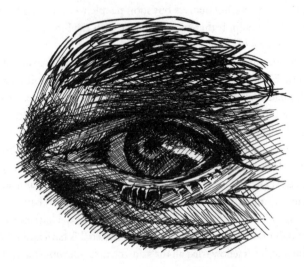

He had been a travelling pedlar, going with his samples from village to village. But he had been stopped in his tracks. Everything of value was taken and his body had been dragged to a crude burial, weighted by boulders and capped with turfs which were now all sewn together. He could only rest if he found someone to listen to his story. At last he had found that person.

By way of thanks, the voice told the listener he would soon find a red stone in a ditch on his very own croft. If he lifted that, he would find what looked like the tooth of a sheep. But this was the tooth of a fairy dog. If he held on to that it would give him special powers and proof would appear very soon, a mark he would bear for the rest of his days.

The bright glow faded then and the voice was gone. Only the soft lapping of a benign sea and the high call of the oystercatcher could be heard. Maybe he was preoccupied but, when he came to their own house, Alasdair failed to bend low enough and his head took a crack from the lintel stone. It bled, but not for long. A wart appeared on his forehead and that always did remain with him.

The very next day he spotted the red stone, lifted it and did indeed find an unusual tooth. It looked more like the back tooth of a horse than anything you'd find in a dog's jaw. Alasdair was already a bit of an authority on crofting matters but soon people were coming from far and wide for help. If there was difficulty with calving or lambing, he would know what to do.

But one time he had a grievance with a fellow who insulted him because he thought he had put too low a value on his croft when his advice had been sought. 'They call you a seer. You can't see the value of the ground that's under your nose.' After that outburst, the same fellow had a run of bad luck with his stock.

Alasdair knew if he used the gift against someone he would lose the power altogether. So he had to make amends. In the next few years, seven calves were born to that man's cow. So the difference was made up.

There came a time when a neighbour, cutting peats on Lamb Island, got a sprinkling of dry peat-dust (*smoor*) in his eye. That's one of the most painful irritations you can get. The material is hard and irregular and acidic. This fellow tried all the known cures –the upper eyelid over the lower one before sneezing; walking into the wind; bathing the eye in this and that. Nothing helped.

Finally someone suggested he should see old Alasdair, who was by then known as the Wizard of Holm. He was a bit disappointed though, because the wise man merely thanked him for his visit and asked him to walk home by the same way and be patient. 'But,' Alasdair said, 'if by any chance your eye improves, by the time you're back, be sure and let me know so I can leave off the treatment.'

The poor fellow walked towards his home across at the head of Broad Bay, but he had only gone halfway when he blinked and felt relief. He waited a moment to make sure and then turned on his heel to thank Alasdair, as he'd promised.

When he bent under the low lintel, he could see Alasdair seated at a small deal table beside the partition that led to the byre. There was a full basin of water in front of him and a thin wooden peg in his hand.

'You're back, I see,' said Alasdair. 'Take a look at this.'

He pointed with the peg. Small dark fragments of peat were floating on the surface.

References
The Wizard of Holm is described in Donald MacDonald, *Tales and Traditions of The Lews* (Birlinn, Edinburgh, 2009). This story is based mainly on the account given by Kenneth MacDonald in *Peat Fire Memories* (Tuckwell Press, 2003). This is an excellent memoir and catches both changing ways of life and timeless stories. My account is also indebted to the eloquent visitors to the Coastguard lookout at Holm Point.

See also John MacLeod, *When I Heard the Bell: The Loss of the Iolaire* (Birlinn, Edinburgh, 2009); Tormod Dòmhnallach, *Call na h-Iolaire* (Acair, Stornoway, 1978); Norman Malcolm MacDonald, *Portrona* (Birlinn, Edinburgh, 2000).

An Apprentice Seaman

Not yesterday nor the day before, there was a young lad who had the great misfortune to lose both his father and his mother when he was young. He was their firstborn and his care was passed to an uncle who was married but had not so far been blessed with a son of his own. I think it's fair to say the lad had a good upbringing. They all lived close to the shore at Sandwick. This village rolls down to the natural harbour which makes up the bay of Stornoway. The boy could see the fishing fleet come and go. He could see the sails of trading ships as they found the breezes to take them past the *Sgeir Mhor* reef, and ghost right in close to the piers.

The boy was given a lot of scope and soon was so handy around the sea that he was allowed the use of a small rowing punt belonging to his uncle. He rowed out one day to a ship which had furled her sails to drop anchor. He had his line aboard and was on deck in an instant. His energy knew no bounds. He took a jump up aloft with the sailors. He saw what they did and was soon running back and fore across the great yard that went across the main mast.

The captain saw all this but did not get angry at the Sandwick lad. 'I think you've an interest in ships, young fellow. How would you like to be apprenticed to this one?'

'I'd like that fine,' he said. People brought up close to the town spoke English as well as Gaelic, even in those days.

'Well you'd better go and ask your father and maybe I could have a word with him. You'd be bound to us for a full five years.'

The boy explained he'd been brought up by his uncle. That was the man to speak to. He was ashore before the ship had settled to her anchor and back again before long after that. His uncle would row out to the ship that very night, but he'd said he thought an apprenticeship at sea could be the making of a lad.

'And did he say what he'd let you go for? What you should ask for wages?'

'He said I should ask to be paid a half-penny at the end of the first month.'

'I think the ship could stretch to that.'

'And could that be two half-pennies at the end of the second?'

'It could.'

'And could that be doubled the same way at the end of each month till the five years is served?'

The captain laughed at the boy, bargaining as instructed, and agreed without thinking much further. He asked him his name and the boy said he was John. Folk usually called him Black John Sandwick, even though he had fair hair. John's uncle came aboard to satisfy himself that his fit nephew would be well looked after. He was sad to lose his company but he knew that those who have a taste for the sea will never settle to anything else till they've given the sailor's life a try.

It will be no surprise to learn that the lad set himself to every task that was shown him with a will he'd never been able to show for his schoolwork at home. He could tie a bowline behind his back and splice three-strand rope. He mastered the plain and the sailmaker's whipping and grew handy with server and mallet. He was first up aloft when sails had to be reefed or let go, but was canny and sure-footed with it. In short, the years and the miles passed quickly. One day the same captain realised that his apprentice was soon to be a fully fledged sailor.

As it happened, they were entering a port in England. The owners were to come aboard to take a glass and inspect the ship, which had made a decent, profitable trade. They asked how the stray cat from Stornoway was doing and the captain said that he'd been taken by surprise to find that the five years were almost up.

'And has the lad proved himself?'

'He's completed every task we've set him, gets on well with his ship-mates. We'd be very sorry to lose him.'

'We'd better pay him what you promised. I suppose he's just had a bob or two to pay his own way ashore. What was your bargain?'

The owners were horrified when the captain told them what he'd agreed to. He never had put it down on paper and calculated what they'd owe. The owners said it was more than the ship was worth and more than it could make from the time her keel was laid to when she was fence posts or firewood.

They did not want to break a bargain made on their behalf but they could not afford to pay the full reckoning. 'We'll gather what ready money we can but it can't be enough. This is what you'll do. Be sure that the ship is well offshore when the lad's time is served. Then offer him what we'll give you, on condition that he takes it at once and that he takes it off the ship along with himself.'

On the eve of the end of the agreed period of five years, the ship was indeed a long way from land. The captain called John at ten in the evening of his last day as apprentice and showed him three bags of coin. There was one of gold, one of silver and one of copper. 'These three are yours if you take them with you off the ship, the minute your apprenticeship is complete,' he said.

Black John Sandwick had picked up some of his uncle's wit. 'Fine,' he said, 'but since you've made one condition, I should be allowed one too.'

'What would that be?'

'Two hours of the carpenter's time.'

'You've served the ship well. We can grant you that and some timber into the bargain.'

By midnight the lad had a raft. It was lowered to the sea and the three bags passed down to him. The captain also passed down a bottle of some drink and that was that.

Morning came and there was no sight of any land. He rigged a simple sail but could only go where the wind was pushing him. By nightfall he knew fear. He took a swig from the bottle and managed to sleep a restless sleep. At the end of the second day there was still no sign of anything but sea and it was a steep and angry territory. Again he took some comfort in a swig from the bottle and gained some rest. But, on the evening of the third day at sea, he spied a wooded coast.

The raft came ashore on a sandy beach. The tide was high, so the water lapped up close to the trees. He managed to drag it ashore and secured it, hidden amongst the branches. He might need it again or it might prove useful for another soul. He found fresh water and some rest. Then he took care to bury each of the three bags in a spot he could mark before he set out to explore.

Black John was fit and strong but he was nearly exhausted by the time he came to a sign of human life. It was a house of stone. There was a wisp of smoke coming from the roof. He chapped on the rough wooden door. A woman came to it, brushing the flour from her apron. She got a shock when she saw the state he was in, from three days adrift on the open sea. First she said he couldn't stay there a minute. Then she took pity on him and fetched water and bread and some fish of some sort. That brought some strength back to him.

'But you can't stay a minute longer here,' she said. 'I serve seven masters and they will kill you as soon as look at you.' She told the boy she had been taken prisoner by a robber gang, to cook and keep house for them. They treated her well enough but they were thieves by trade. The lad said he did not have the strength to walk a step further but she wasn't to worry, he could take care of himself. He fell into a deep sleep, stretched out by the fire.

He woke to a shouting and bawling. 'Good evening, gentlemen,' he said, 'Could I have a word with your leader?' They all looked to each other because this was a gang with no leader. They told him they were robbers to trade and they could have no witnesses to that. They were home to share out the spoils of their work.

'And how did you get on today?'

'No harm in you taking a look,' one of them said, 'The chink of this silver is the last thing you'll ever see.' But then this bold lad said, 'Is that all you earned today, between the lot of you?' They were taken aback. He told them that thievery was his own chosen trade.

'Tell you what,' he went on, 'I can show you how to make some real money. I bet you I can thieve more than any of you can, three day's running.'

Some of them were for killing him, at once, for his cheek but some of them couldn't resist a bet. Soon they were squabbling until one did say, 'I'm fed up of having to argue about everything. This lad looks like he's been in a scrape or two. If he can do better than any of us for three days, he should be our leader.'

They all set out, some in pairs and some alone, and all returned at dusk. A meagre haul of trinkets and coins was gathered by the fire. Then the Stornoway lad placed his heavy bag of coppers on the ground and he'd topped them all, by far. The next day of course, he produced the silver. But no one could argue on the third day when he returned with the bag of gold. He was made chief there and then.

So he did not have to forage on the fourth day but said he'd start to get the affairs of the outpost in order while his men did their best, out in the world. It was then he discovered that the poor soul who kept house had a key always at her belt. She had showed him the store of grain and the store of treasure but she had not shown him any door which could be opened with that key. He asked and she protested but she couldn't argue when he pointed out that he was now the unanimously elected chief. She took him to an outhouse, a little down a path, concealed by branches.

When the key was turned, a most pitiful sight was revealed. There, suspended by her hair, was a poor young woman, stretched so her feet hardly touched the ground. He cut her down from the rafter and found that she still had some breath in her body. Between the housekeeper and the captive, the lad discovered that this was the daughter of the king of Spain. Two of the robbers had been caught at her father's palace and been put to death. This was the revenge of the remaining gang of seven. They had captured the king's daughter and now tortured her in this way.

Before the end of the day, this beautiful young woman had revived sufficiently to flee with the man who had freed her. First they made a show of tying the housekeeper to a chair so none could guess that she had helped. Then they took as much of the gold as they could carry and soon they were off, into the woods.

By good fortune they came upon a shelter before they were completely exhausted. It was no more than a bothy – a bit like the bare dwellings of stone, back on the Lewis moorland, where people went with their cattle and sheep for the summer grazings. But that was enough to hide them for now. The daughter of the king of Spain closed her eyes at once but the lad kept his ears open as he wrapped her in his sailor's jacket. He heard the scratching of animals and he heard something that might be human. He feared it was the robbers already and crept out to take them on.

But it was a sight that scared him more than the seas which had tossed his simple raft. There was not one but three unhappy ghosts. There was no wailing to be heard for neither of them had a head on his shoulders. But each made a pathetic scratching and pointing. He knew they were seeking help and he followed where each one walked. There were a few bony gestures and soon that sharp young man had found a head for each set of shoulders. This was three travellers, murdered by the same gang of robbers. They could find no peace till they had had found the heads which had been severed from them. Now each could lie in the ferns and moss and take their rest.

With that favour done, it was time the fugitives were on their way. After many close shaves and lucky escapes, they at last reached the safety of a bustling seaport. They had left most of the fortune behind but still had more than enough gold to find good lodgings. They were still a long way from a place either of them could call home territory. It will be no surprise that the dark-haired young woman fell in love with her rescuer and he also thought he could do a lot worse for himself. They were married and soon had their own house and healthy business. Money makes money, as the uncle of the time-served apprentice had taught him.

All was going well until a ship of the Spanish flag dropped anchor in that bay. The captain came ashore for provisions and his sharp eye recognised the missing princess. There was, of course, a huge reward for anyone who could bring her home alive to her family – in fact, the customary half a kingdom and hand of said daughter. The couple thought it would be much simpler to keep their identities secret. They had plenty to live on and these robbers would still be hunting for a certain Black John, though they did not know his name or city of origin. The captain gave no sign that he knew the true identity of this shopkeeper's wife but made a show of polite trading. Of course the couple were invited to dine aboard. They accepted, suspecting nothing.

While they were sipping wine, tasting cheese and listening to a lively guitar, Black John jumped from the table with a start. He knew when a ship was underway. The anchor had been hauled silently. This time, it was themselves who had been tricked. Despite the pleas of his wife, he was set adrift in a tiny ship's boat with neither oar nor sail. Again, he was completely at the mercy of the elements. Again, he was given only one bottle of drink. Again, he rationed himself to a swig at night so he could gain some rest. But this time, on the third day, there was no sign of any land. Even Black John was close to despair.

It was right then that a very strange phenomenon took a grip of the tiny vessel. The painter which had fallen into the sea was stretched out ahead. To his surprise, John also saw that there was a trackline of small bubbles at the stern. Somehow the boat was being driven through the sea. At first he thought he was in the grip of a strong ocean current. Then he realised the track was steady and he was being pulled with a purpose. Before another day had passed, he caught a glimpse of the clouds which indicated high ground under them. As the dinghy came close to a lonely beach, he could make out three dim shapes, staggering out of the sea. Of course the three souls he'd helped to their rest had risen to repay the favour.

Black John was ashore again. His good clothes were torn and he had not a penny in his pocket but he still had his wits and his strength and a good Scots tongue in his head. He thanked his rescuers and found a path to the nearest town. It was a great day in that country, which happened to be Spain.

The long-lost daughter of the king was to be married to the captain who had rescued her. She protested of course but her father said a deal was a deal and he didn't really have a choice. She had negotiated only one slim chance to find her own true Lewisman, if he was still alive by some twist of fate. Each man in the kingdom had the chance to walk by, under her balcony, in case she should recognise a poor, weather-beaten survivor.

Lewis folk are not always noted for their prompt timekeeping, but it really was very close to the setting of the sun when a sweating and breathless fair-haired fellow did indeed pass again into her field of vision. This was her own Black John Sandwick. He was given the hand that already was his own and neither wanted for anything again.

I have no information on any future adventures, births or voyages but we can surely imagine that John sailed his bride up the road to the Hebrides so his good lady could meet the man who had made such a good bargain for his nephew, back before all the events of these swiftly passing years.

References

Collected and retold by the Revd James MacDougall (John Grant, Edinburgh, 1910). Full text: https://archive.org/stream/folktales-fairylo 01macd#page/94/mode/2up. See also *Highland Fairy Legends*, collected James MacDougall, ed. Calder with a new intro by Alan Bruford, D S Brewer, Cambridge, 1978 (this edition omits the longer tales like this one).

MacDougall firmly roots the story in the port of Stornoway, then a bustling centre of international trade. It combines elements of the widespread tradition of the island boy who goes to sea and has adventures with elements of international folk tales. I'd compare it with 'The Captain of the Black Ship', from Angus John MacPhail of Loch Eport, North Uist, transcribed and translated in Bruford and MacDonald. Similar adventures are in J.F. Campbell's collection of *Popular Tales of the West Highlands*. This one could also be termed a fortune tale of the type where a princess is saved from slavery, but it also has elements of tales of seven robbers collected by the brothers Grimm and the key suggests the Bluebeard tales, like Mr Fox, alluded to in Shakespeare.

It invites comparison with the sea-maid story in J.F. Campbell's collection – several versions from different Gaelic-speaking areas – as this also contains elements of the winning of the princess and the repaying of favours by three creatures helped along the way.

As Bruford remarks, it's a pity that MacDougall does not acknowledge his sources in any detail. However, MacDougall's retellings are clear, strong examples of storytelling, perhaps like Dasent's translations of Norwegian tales, and they avoid the flourishes and wordy padding that many retellings of 'Celtic' tales resort to.

AN ENCOUNTER

It was back in the time of the steam-drifters. There was coal, piled high around the harbour. Barrowloads of it going along planks to the boats. You could walk across the width of Stornoway harbour on their decks.

This time, a fellow from the Point district, a *Rudhach*, went on the ran-dan. He had a hell of a skinful, no chance of making the bus home. So his instinct prevailed and he found a warm place for himself. What he didn't know was that he'd found his way on to one of the boats. There was still heat in the boiler and he was stretched out on the coals beside it.

Of course, no one saw him there and the crew came-to, to fire her up at first light. Now the men from Point, they've this way of talking. Whatever they're going to say, it's *a ghràidh* this and *a ghràidh* that. It means 'my dear' but it's just a way of speaking and you'll hear a man say that to another man.

So the stoker is giving it welly, digging into the heap and shovelling away. He sees this body stretched out there and gets the shock of his life. He says, 'Where in the middle of hell did you spring from?'

The *Rudhach* has woken up now and his head's banging, the thirst is raging and he's seen the wiry stoker, stripped to the waist, nothing but his eyes shining in a face full of soot.

'Oh, well, Satan, *a ghràidh*, when I was alive I was from Point.'

Told to me by David Jardine, who was born and brought up in Stornoway. This was after I delivered a storytelling session at Ullapool Book Festival in 2007. There is no separation between performers and audience at this wonderful event and this was the ideal situation where stories suggested others once the ball was rolling.

FROM FATHER AND MOTHER

It's all too easy to take your parents' work and skills for granted. My father, John B, was a grocer by trade and manager of the first Lipton's shop in Stornoway. He was proud of his ability to bone a side of ham with minimum waste. I can see him putting a black-handled knife to a steel. Then he'd let the blade fall along the bone. I'm only now realising what a natural storyteller he was. He was from the Doric-speaking north-east of the Scottish mainland and he would recreate the character of an uncle famous for breaking in horses that no one else could go near. I also remember him repeating stories he'd heard in the busy shop or incidents that tickled his sense of humour. Soon these became set-piece stories.

Lipton's ran a fleet of vans – green-painted mobile shops which served the rural areas of Lewis and Harris. My father was always moaning about the extra book-keeping but he got on well with some of the drivers. I remember Loyn as a short man who always wore a beret. My father said he was a real poacher, both salmon and deer. He turned a blind eye to what Loyn was selling under the counter. But he said that Loyn was deaf as a post – maybe more from shooting at deer than from anything that happened in the war.

So he nagged at the driver to go and see about getting a hearing-aid. 'You're entitled to one and you're needing one, dealing with the public.' Sure enough, the driver noticed the difference. 'Best thing since sliced bread,' he said.

But the next time my father spoke to him he had to shout as usual. The hearing-aid was missing.

'What happened to it? I thought you were getting on with it all right.'

LIPTON

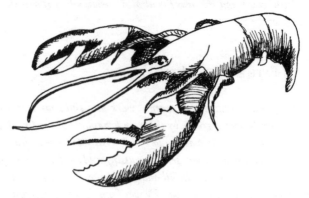

'So I was,' says Loyn. 'It was great in the van, hearing what everyone was asking for, instead of guessing. But see the first time I took it to the river. I used to be brave as a lion. With that thing on, I could hear my own footsteps. Every shake of the heather. I was nervous as hell. Twitchy. So I threw the thing in the river.'

My mother, Johann, was a bonny, petite woman with tight curly hair. She was very active, always baking or knitting or sewing. She was famous in the family for her wit. She would recite gently satirical verses at family gatherings. I used to like holding hanks of oily wool for her while she expertly made perfect balls of wool for knitting. She would entertain you while you helped her. Sometimes Johann would translate Gaelic sayings for me.

'You're a big fisherman now so you should know what the three fastest things in the sea are?'

I would read every angling book and sea story I could get hold of then so my reply would have been something like, 'I'm guessing, the sailfish, the marlin and the bluefin tuna.'

'Not around these waters,' she said. 'There's a Gaelic saying that the three fastest in the sea are the seal, the mackerel and the lobster.'

I might have guessed the mackerel. I often felt their power on the end of a line, but I was thinking of the fat harbour seals, wallowing about as they lazily took their choice of what was thrown over when the trawlers were gutting their catch. She let me have a few words before giving me her argument.

'If you catch a mackerel, you can feel the rate it goes zig-zagging through the water. If a seal is chasing that mackerel, it will take it from your hook. Therefore it must be faster. But if you can snatch it aboard first, and use it for bait, you might see the fastest of all. Just watch the movement of the catching claw of the lobster when it comes out of the creel. You don't want to let your fingers get in the way of that.'

There is an extra twist, given by time, during my own life period. In 2013 a bluefin tuna of over 500 pounds was caught on rod and line out near Hyskeir. I thought of the saying taught to me by my mother. But I know that she would have argued that the tuna is very closely related to the mackerel anyhow so she would hold by her tradition.

SMITH'S SHOE SHOP

On Bayhead, Stornoway, you could enter the retail section of a shoe shop which had men's and women's departments and connected through to a back shop. But you entered the 'University of Kenneth Street' from the back door which led more directly into the workshop. There always seemed to be a kettle boiling and you wonder how any shoes ever got resoled. But it was much the same at Calum Stealag, the blacksmiths, where folk came in for a heat. And out of town, at Port of Ness, Norman 'Gagan' MacLeod told me he often wondered how his father managed to complete one boat, never mind the hundreds which left the yard.

I can remember how the whir of the sewing machine chimed with the banter. I'm sure the three brothers, now retired, would not mind me telling one yarn linked to the family business.

There was a fellow joined the Naval Reserve and had a few meeks and wings in his pooch (ha'pennies and pennies in his pocket). So he went into Smith's Shoe Shop and left his best shoes to get soled and heeled. 'Come back in a week,' the fellow at the counter said.

'Aye, all right.' But it was right then that war broke out. Since he was in the Reserve, he got his call-up right away and he was off.

You could write a whole book about what happened to him over the next six years. I don't remember how many times he was torpedoed. He was in cold seas and in warm seas but he always got hauled into a lifeboat and he came through it. But he happened to be in New Zealand at the end of the war and the climate suited him fine.

He made a living there for a couple of years but the old magnetic rock of the Island of Lewis was pulling at him. He had to get back and see a few of the old family while they were still alive. He joined a ship and worked his passage and had a few experiences along the way. Eventually he boarded the ferry at Kyle of Lochalsh – a fine new ship called the *Loch Seaforth* – and that was him home.

Next day he was walking down Bayhead to the hoil (harbour) when he realised he was wearing the same tweed jacket he had when he was last home. It had been waiting for him on a peg in the family house. He reached deep in a pocket and pulled out the old blue cobbler's ticket.

Just on the off-chance, he walked round to Kenneth Street and handed the ticket over at the desk. 'I don't suppose there's any chance you've got these tucked away anywhere,' he said.

The old fellow put his glasses on and took a good look. 'Hang on,' he said, as he got on a stepladder and reached up, right to the end of the top shelf. He picked up a pair of shoes and looked at the ticket on them. Then he said, from the ladder, 'Tell you what, can you come back in a week for them?'

I heard this yarn from the playwright Eric MacDonald, who lives in the Uig area. As lead artist in The Sail Loft Project, Stornoway, 2005, I commissioned and directed a short play, which was produced as a promenade performance through the restored building, now used as housing. The funny but thoughtful script by Eric MacDonald included a version of this tale.

LOOKING WHERE YOU'RE GOING

I grew up in very good quality council housing in the town of Stornoway. My mother, Johann, was a Gaelic speaker but Gaelic was only spoken in the house when her brothers and sisters or neighbours were in and they wanted to discuss something the children were too young to hear. Often there would be much chortling and giggling and then I'd pester my mother or aunt till they gave me a translation. Very often they only shook their heads and said it just could not be told in English.

A few years later, an elderly friend of mine, recently come to live on the island, visited the exhaust installer to get some welding done on his classic Austin A35. The fellow down the pit, who I knew to be cheery and charming, began to talk in Gaelic to the fellow passing down the bits.

My friend told me he asked politely if they wouldn't mind speaking in a language he could understand, as it was his exhaust which was under discussion.

'No, we can't do that,' the welder said. 'English is too poor a language to describe the state of your bloody exhaust system.'

I mention this to try to dispel the idea that all stories from the Western Isles are full of gloom. We do like our premonitions and tragedies but I think there is an equally strong strand of storytelling in quoting witty retorts and enjoying the behaviour of fairly outrageous characters who seem to get away with being a bit different.

My mother told many stories of her great-uncle Donald Campbell. Her brother Calum Smith published his account of this man as a chapter in Around The Peat Fire. *I published some short stories, largely based on these family stories, back in 1981, but usually I prefer to tell them, to show this other strand of the sort of tales we like to tell this part of the world.*

Very early on I found that one such yarn leads to the next. My mother's story of Donald Campbell on the fishing boat is a completely different story to the one Calum retold in his own book, and no doubt there are dozens of variations.

I do remember telling a string of them to an Arthritis Association gathering at the Retirement Centre in Stornoway. People kept coming up to me afterwards and telling me of things they'd been reminded of. I have no note of the teller's name but I do remember one of these replies. It also proves the point that not all stories from the Western Isles are of epic proportions.

There was a fellow in our family could easily have been a second cousin of your own relation. He got himself organised and went everywhere on a BSA bicycle. He even got himself a front light. Ever Ready. But he was still stopped by the cops who told him the law obliged him to carry a red light at the rear. 'A rear light,' he says. 'I want to see where I'm going. I know where I'm coming from.'

References

For recollections of Donald Campbell and some of his sayings, see Calum Smith, *Around the Peat Fire* (Birlinn, Edinburgh, 2001). My own retelling of Donald Campbell stories was updated in *Mackerel and Creamola* (Polygon pocketbooks, Edinburgh, 2001 and still available from an Lanntair, Stornoway; The Ceilidh Place bookshop, Ullapool; The Fruitmarket Gallery, Edinburgh).

NORTH LEWIS

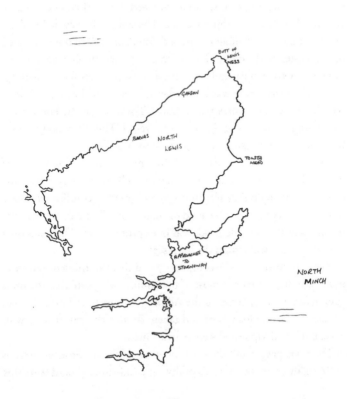

A DISAPPEARANCE

There was a smith in every clan and later in every township, so it's no sur-prise that there are a large number of families of that name in the Western Isles. That happened to be my mother's maiden name, usually in its Gaelic form (Nic a' Ghobhainn or, for a man, Mac a' Ghobhainn). People throughout the Outer Hebrides usually like to find out who your people are and which townships you have family links with. A few times a story has been passed to me because folk have known my mother's people. This is a tradition, clearly based on an actual incident.

It was in the village of Galson, in the Ness district, in the mid-1800s. Like all other villages in Lewis and Harris, the people needed to work on the sea as well as on the land to feed themselves. This was always a risky enterprise, as open boats were launched from surf-beaches, to cope with the Atlantic. The fishing was rich. The cod and ling could be salted, dried and sold. The halibut or turbot did not cure well so this was shared out and eaten fresh. It must have been a very welcome change from the monotonous diet of oat and barley meal, milk, potatoes and salt herring.

They say that there was no market for the huge 'barn door' skate which would sometimes take a hook. These would be laid on the shore, under the keel of the returning vessel. The slimy body would help them slide the stout boat up above the tide line.

There are many records of sad drownings, often within sight of home. But this was something different. The Galson boat was dis-covered, drifting out at sea, in very good weather conditions. There were no signs of damage by wind or rogue wave. The oars were on the thwarts and the gear and tackle was in its proper place. There was only one clue. A cap was left on the stern seat.

The superstitious in the community said that this thing or the other must have happened but most of the families were sure that the press gang had struck. A vessel of the Admiralty must have lowered a gig, chased the beamy local boat and taken these men against their will. Several of the disappeared were married men.

The years passed and there was no word of any of those taken from their small craft. In those days, living conditions aboard warships

were terrible. Men could die of disease or neglect even before they'd met the savage splinters caused by enemy fire.

At that time, in the Hebrides, it was hardly possible for a widow to make a life on her own. It was backbreaking work, building up any depth of soil for cultivation and carrying seaweed from the shore to nourish the peaty ground. And this woman already had children to look after. There was an agreed period of time to go through. After that, a man could be presumed to be no longer living, if no word was heard. A widow was then free to remarry and start a new life. Often a brother or cousin of a missing man – a bachelor or a widower – would take responsibility for his relation's widow.

I cannot say if it was from love or necessity or both but after the slow passing of lean and hungry years, the widow of the man who had left only a cap behind him was indeed remarried. They were happy enough and soon the family grew and they all managed to make a living for themselves.

One day, years and years after the drifting boat was discovered, a stranger was seen in the village. He asked after the 'widow' by her maiden name and by her first married name. The person he spoke to did not recognise this weather-beaten man and thought he must be a 'tinker' or travelling tinsmith. But he was pointed to the croft of the woman's new husband.

One of the children thought they saw a face at the window that night. When the door was opened, no one was waiting there.

My friend Mary Smith tells me that it was her own great-grandmother who became a bigamist. It seems that the sailor had survived and returned at last to his home village. He knew at a glance he could not pick up the fibres of his own life but had to make a new one. So Mary recalls how two strands of the family would meet at family funerals. It was always a bit awkward. The children would ask why these other people were there. They didn't recognise them as relatives.

References
Told to me by Mary Smith (Màiri Nic a' Ghobhainn) in *an Lanntair*, Stornoway, during Faclan book festival, 2013. Bill Lawson also summarises the story in his *Lewis, the West Coast in History and Legend* (Birlinn, Edinburgh, 2008, p. 62). Mary is a powerful and sensitive singer, a visual artist, an educator and a bearer of countless traditions in song and story: see www.capefarewell.com/seachange/wild-gaelic/ and www.seachd.com/pages/music_vocalists.html.

THE TWO BROTHERS

One story leads to the next, sometimes suggested by geography, as markers along a journey, and sometimes by theme or phrase. The next link in the chain of stories is a tradition that takes us further north, up the coastline of Lewis. There are still a few living veterans of the great-line fishing which took place out in the open ocean from beamy vessels launched from the shores of North Lewis. The history of that fishery, the vessels created for it and the successes and tragedies linked to it may well produce a book in its own right. No collection of Western Isles stories could be complete without at least one account.

When they began to build the large class of *sgoth Niseach*, measuring over 30 feet overall, some said they would make many widows. Men now had the means to venture even further out into the open waters, in search of a livelihood and an adventure. Sometimes the men had little say in it. The vessels and tackle were supplied by the laird, seeing a good market for dried fish of the first quality.

But sometimes a crew worked their way up, investing their profits until they could run a larger seaworthy boat. Two brothers each became a skipper of a *sgoth* of about 25 feet overall. Some said the boats were as like as the lads.

One year the two vessels went together, under sail, to the outlying island of Sula Sgeir. That bare grey rock lies about 40 miles north-north-east of the Butt of Lewis. Somehow these beamy boats were hauled up, off the water, to be secured in a geo – little more than a crack in the rock. The crews stayed in a simple stone bothy for a fortnight, taking a harvest of the young gannets, or *guga*, caught just before they were able to fly the nest.

A team still makes that journey every year and the work has hardly changed. There's not much romance about it and the men themselves call it a factory, as the birds are plucked, singed and salted. Not so many years back, this catch was a vital part of the community's survival.

Each of these brothers must have been well respected because the skipper was elected by the rest of the crew. When the work was done, the boats were relaunched and loaded with the catch of birds and the gear they would take home.

A savage squall hit, just when the vessels were leaving the shelter of the bay. Once you're out of that, you're exposed to the full weight of weather and sea, hurled over many miles of exposed ocean.

By chance, the skippers had chosen to hoist sail on a different tack. When the wind is more or less behind you that is a possibility. Once they were running, neither could afford to attempt to change the yard and sail over to the other side. That manoeuvre can take some time in challenging conditions and the *sgoth* would be powerless for that period, and so at the mercy of the building waves.

So each brother wisely held to the tack and course he was on. You could see nothing of the other vessel but the top part of its sail when it was lost in a trough of the swell. When each boat rose at the same time, the brothers both held a hand up in the air as a farewell. Each knew it might be the last glimpse he had of his brother and his vessel.

It was a mainly northerly wind with biting hail in it even though it was not yet September. Visibility was poor and it was a mercy when Cape Wrath lighthouse showed for one of the brothers, still at the helm. On the other *sgoth*, his brother had his bowman look out for the flash of the Butt of Lewis light.

The brother making for Cape Wrath was alert for every second, even though he was exhausted from reading the seas which were driving them so fast. His crew wanted him to keep on going to enter the North Minch, but he knew that the worst seas would be close to the headland. He sensed they had the tide with them and he took advantage of that and turned her along the north coast of Scotland.

They made their landfall at Loch Eriboll. The boat hit the beach with a surge but they'd all come through it, and all came ashore unharmed.

The most dangerous part of any voyage is often close to home. People tend to drop their guard when they recognise the marks that take them to a known harbour. The crew of the brother making for Butt of Lewis tried to persuade their skipper to turn into Port of Ness. But he knew that there would be a dangerous swell and confused seas when they hit the counter-currents close to harbour.

So this brother held her well out to sea, a few miles clear of the turbulent water near to the lighthouse. They ran on down the Atlantic coast of Lewis, all through the night. At last, on the second day, they could gain the shelter of Loch Roag.

The *Siarach* folk (Westsiders) were amazed to see the North Lewis *sgoth* arrive out of the open Atlantic in such conditions.

Both brothers brought their vessels to safety by holding to the course they were on. There's not many Lewis sea stories have a happy ending like this one.

This tradition was passed on to me by Alasdair Smith, like John D. Smith a master mariner and also a coastguard colleague of mine at the time. He told it as a village story he'd heard and again I took no notes but the narrative line was so strong that I was able to continue passing it on. By this time we worked in a modern operations room, bristling with information technology.

Some of the detail comes from my own experience of sailing sgoth Niseach. *In 2010, I had the pleasure of skippering the last surviving example of a working* sgoth, *Jubilee (1935) from Stornoway to Port of Ness and out from there to Sula Sgeir. After returning to port, we found another weather window which allowed us to sail non-stop to Stromness, Orkney.* Jubilee *is 27ft overall so I can say, first hand, that the routes outlined in this story are completely feasible for these seaworthy vessels. Our voyage to Sula Sgeir is described by Robert MacFarlane in* The Old Ways *(now available in Penguin paperback, 2013).*

Jubilee was built by John Finlay MacLeod, the man who swam with the rope from the grounded Iolaire *on New Year's night, 1919. She was renovated and restored to her original rig by his son John Murdo MacLeod in the late 1970s. She remains in active use as a community boat.*

You can support her and other Hebridean sailing craft such as a recreation of the larger sgoth Niseach, *an* Sulaire, *by joining* Falmadair, *the North Lewis Maritime Society (www.falmadair.com).*

A Fertile Island

We have it on good authority that the Steward of St Kilda made his way out to Hirta (*Hiort*) in a spell of fair weather, well into the season. There was something very unusual about this visit, in that his good lady was there with him. She had always wanted to set foot on these volcanic islands which broke the skyline out from mainland Harris. She had her wish this time, though they had their adventures on the way.

The sea was thick with herring, on the passage out. In the frenzy of feeding, a plunging gannet dived through the planking of their beamy open boat. Its own beak stopped the gap and the vessel sailed on to make its landing in Village Bay. Some of the sailors said that this was not a good omen for the return voyage.

It was a simple repair. That and the other business was done and the vessel set out again for the one-day crossing back through the Sound of Harris. But that's not the way they went. A gale came at them, from the south, not long after they'd left the shadow of the archipelago. The lady had pleaded to come along, against the skipper's feelings, and, to her credit, she never moaned.

They were drenched in rain and spray and held on fearfully as the craft surfed on. They were being driven northwards, beyond any chance of reaching the Sound. That night they got a glimpse of the Seven Hunters which make up the Flannan Isles. Still the southerly blasted and the skipper judged they could not risk these steep waves on their beam to try for Loch Roag.

They took the huge seas on their quarter and streamed all spare cordage over the stern, to slow them as they ran on. They were being driven only by the pressure of the gale on their bare single spar of timber. They might have made out the high shape of Old Hill, out from Great Bernera. That was really their last chance of reaching safe shelter. Still they were driven on, wrapped up in all they had, but still shivering.

Mercifully they were driven at speed so the distance fell away. There are very few shores where you could attempt landfall between East Loch Roag and the Butt of Lewis. So they continued on. Even the more experienced crew pleaded with their skipper to make a try for the shore at Ness, rounding the Butt of Lewis. But that wise man knew to resist even the requests of the Steward. Their best hope was to keep out to deep water and keep that wind where it was.

At last there was the grey high shape of the bare rock of Sula Sgeir. No landfall either. Only the gannet-hunters land there. They pick their day and very rarely leave a boat at anchor for more than a few hours.

Their next hope was the offshore island of North Rona. There was a viable farm on that green-topped stone. It was known to be a fertile place with a yield of grain, as well as mutton and beasts. The battered craft did find shelter there, close to a geo in the rock. They were able to hear themselves again, above the screeching of wind and birds.

They attempted a landing but the heavy vessel was difficult to hold off. There was the sickening sound of splintering planks as they tried to hold her close enough so all the crew and their two important passengers could stumble ashore.

Every person aboard came on to the rock with only a scrape or a graze. It was the skipper who was wincing as his fine skiff took a pounding. They all thought they had reached safety at last. They were expecting to be met by the family who kept the farm out there. But there was no welcome for them. You would have thought these lonely folk would have been glad of a bit of companionship and willing to share what they had been able to put aside, with a winter coming.

The island farm was deathly quiet. When they pushed a door open they found a terrible sight. The family on Rona had perished and their few surviving animals were running wild and desperate. A plague of rats had come ashore down the ropes of a ship tethered in the bay. The store of grain had been eaten and the people had starved.

The survivors who had come from the ocean had an important task to do, once they had recovered themselves. They had to give the remains a decent burial and say some words from The Book.

Then they rallied together and foraged and caught birds and a few fish and somehow found the means of making a poor fire. Everything was shared and there was no account of rank.

The days passed and became months, and still they all held on. One of the crew was a very able carpenter, even though the only tools were the most basic – a hand saw, a long knife and an axe. He gathered what driftwood there was and saved it from the fire. He patched and hewed and whittled. There was mutton fat to make a kind of tallow and a strong thread to bind this and that together. By the time there was relief from the high winds, he had rebuilt their craft so it would float again.

They dared not attempt to fight the wind in their strange vessel, but waited until the sky looked fair. All returned to the same craft which had taken them this far. On a cold bright spring morning, they again cast themselves to the mercy of the sea. Their compass was intact. After a day at sea they could make out the lie of the land to the Butt of Lewis, but they would not risk the tricky surf at the beach.

Then there was Tiumpan Head. But the tides boil away off that point. They would have to drive through turbulence before they could gain any shelter. So on they sailed, with a mild wind at the helmsman's shoulder.

They made a good passage, clear of Chicken Rock and on into the natural harbour of Stornoway bay. Coopers and packers and net-menders and shipwrights looked up from their work in amazement. They witnessed one of the strangest arrivals ever seen at that port. The patchwork craft, laden with crew, for none were now passengers, made her arrival. And there was a woman amongst them. The Steward replied to the questions. Bonnets were tilted and heads scratched. The survivors were helped ashore to warm lodgings and nourishing food, while the story spread round the town.

Word was sent at once to family and kin. Of course, memorial ser-vices had already been said for the missing people.

But that's not the end of it. It was always said in the north of Lewis that Rona was the fertile island. So much so that it was rare for a ewe to have one lamb or a cow to drop a single calf. When her time came, they discovered that the human animal was not that different. The twins were both strong healthy sons and one of them was promised at once to the ministry.

The Steward and his wife wanted to return something to the providence which they sensed had taken them through the ordeal. In fact there is a carved motto, recurring through the town of Stornoway, along with the images of a sailing vessel and a shoal of herring: 'God's Providence Is Our Inheritance.'

References
Retold from the Morrison manuscript.

A NOTE ON
THE SOURCES

Many of the stories gathered here have been previously collected, usually in the Gaelic language, then transcribed and translated. These sources are indicated, where known, and I hope the reader will consult original material, such as the publications and recordings held at the School of Scottish Studies, in Edinburgh. Many of these are available through the online resource, *Tobar an Dualchais*.

The collection made by A.J. Bruford and D.A. MacDonald is still in print and it contains a representative grouping of tales, covering the complex geography and linguistic groups of this small country of Scotland. These stories from the Western Isles will fall into place in that wider context. At least six people born or schooled in the Western Isles, have worked for the School and made a huge contribution in collecting material at a crucial point: Donald Archie MacDonald, North Uist, Angus Duncan, from Scarp; John MacInnes, from Uig, Lewis; Morag MacLeod, Scalpay, Harris; Margaret Bennett, who was brought up on Lewis; and Cathlin MacAulay, Great Bernera.

Alexander Carmichael's *Carmina Gadelica* is often overlooked as a source of stories. The fifth volume intersperses collected tales from Barra and Uist, often containing refrains in verse, with the charms associated with healing or protection from troubles. Sometimes the huge body of lore collected by Father Allan MacDonald, the priest on Eriskay in the late nineteenth and early twentieth century, is also overlooked. Traditions relating to second-sight and the supernatural are better known than the religious fables told in the Roman Catholic community of the Western Isles. For a full list of Father MacDonald's publications see http://www.scalan.co.uk/eriskay.htm.

The 1901 collection, *Scottish Fairy and Folk Tales* by George Douglas, is available online. It is fascinating to compare versions of tales from the Western Isles told in these collections with later transcriptions of recorded stories. Take 'The Tale of the Cauldron', from Sandray, for just one example and compare George Douglas's retelling with Nan MacKinnon's, published in the Bruford and MacDonald book. When you move from Nan's version of 'The Man Who Took a Fairy Lover', also in Bruford and MacDonald, to the group of versions gathered by Carmichael, you get a glimpse of the way a natural storyteller remakes a story in the telling, while staying true to its essentials. It does seem that the Outer Hebrides has had more than its fair share of strong tellers, in the same way as oral music is a strong part of our culture.

I would also suggest that keen students of folklore go directly to the Morrison manuscript, published in 1975 by Stornoway Public Library as *Traditions of the Western Isles*. It is out of print but reference and lending copies are held in Stornoway Library and it is also available for reference in the National Library of Scotland. Morrison was a well-read man, working as a cooper in Stornoway in the early 1800s. His accounts of endless clan conflicts also capture a sense of the outlying islands being not yet politically connected with a larger Great Britain. Oral traditions of local feuds alternate with wise and witty stories. A few of these can take their place in an international canon of timeless tales and one of his transcriptions is reproduced in full, with kind permission of Western Isles Libraries, as an appendix.

The work of J.F Campbell and John Lorne Campbell was also essential reading. The former was a friend of Sir George W. Dasent, who translated the seminal *Popular Tales from the Norse*, collected by Peter Christen Asbjørnsen and Jørgen Moe, published in English in 1859. J.F. Campbell worked with a group of collectors to gather, transcribe and translate the stories gathered in *Popular Tales of the West Highlands* and its sequel. I would say his approach was to gather and transcribe tales as heard, rather than remake them into a more coherent but more literary form. In this respect he was ahead of his time, as the method of collecting and transcribing seems in accordance with current practice.

Though John Lorne Campbell was not linked to any university, his adoption of mechanical recorders to preserve original material is very much in line with the work of the field-workers sent out from bodies such as the School of Scottish Studies. His translations and transcriptions of John MacPherson (Coddy) and Angus MacLellan are of huge importance. Often, the published versions form interesting counterpoints to other recordings or oral versions of the same tales. But the work of social historians has also been vital in noting the background and sources of stories and storytelling as well as brief retellings of tales linked to traditions. Donald MacDonald's *Lewis: A History of the Island* and Bill Lawson's *Harris in History and Legend* and its companion volumes on North Uist, West Lewis and East Lewis are thorough studies and all are still in print. The Scottish publisher Birlinn/Polygon, along with its academic imprint of John Donald, has kept existing works available and continued to publish new ones such as Bill Lawson's close scrutiny of culture, from settlement to settlement, through time as well as geography.

John MacAulay's discussion of the Hebridean galley (*Bìrlinn*, The White Horse Press, Cambridge, 1996) gives an informed account of a historical maritime culture behind many of the stories. And his more provocative theories on the seal legends in *Seal Folk and Ocean Paddlers* (White Horse Press, 1998) offer sustained and entertaining arguments.

Doctor Donald MacDonald (*Tales and Traditions of the Lews*, first published in 1967 and also reissued by Birlinn) retells tales from the Morrison manuscript and updates these with accounts of more recent historical events, such as the local take on the Land Raid riots which took place on Lewis. But amongst a very mixed bag of tales and verses there is the tragic story of the men from Mealasta, assembled from several oral sources.

I have been able to access the work of current collectors, in this case Maggie Smith and Chrisella Ross, whose recordings have added telling details to well-known tales like this one. And Bill Lawson reprints Donald S. Murray's translation of the tragic song which, as so often in Gaelic culture, compresses a story on a huge scale into a few verses. Maggie and Chrisella, both native Gaelic speakers, are fine storytellers in their own right and both have been generous in sharing their findings and their experience.

Storytelling has always been a two-way trade. Mainland Scottish travellers like Duncan Williamson attribute several of their tales to tellers from the Western Isles. In turn, the influence of travellers or itinerant tinsmiths, or 'tinkers', is left in stories imported into the islands. Carmichael relates his meeting with an impressive MacDonald family on Barra. He retells a strange tale told in the lines of a ballad sung by Isabella MacDonald. Generations on, John MacInnes recorded Peter Stewart, settled in Barvas, Lewis, relating his version of the international tale of the clever peasant girl.

As well as the huge range of published texts, I am equally indebted to a host of remembered conversations. Some of these were with writers who have published their own works influenced by Western Isles folklore, such as Norman Malcolm MacDonald and Francis Thompson. But many of my sources are previously unrecorded. I was lucky enough to be born on the Island of Lewis, just before the coming of the television. Village ways continued in the cul-de-sacs of Stornoway and I would also be taken out of town to join the 'relations' at peat-cutting or sheep-fanks. But, along with nearly all my contemporaries in the town, I was not taught Gaelic, though it was my mother's first language. I have gratefully taken advice from those who are competent in that language and have thus given me access to material I would never have known.

But it's a mistake to think that there are no longer any tellers who have both the knowledge of traditional tales and the skills to make them memorable. In 2005 I was honoured to be in the crew of the community boat *Sealladh* which took Angus (Moy) MacDonald back to the Monach islands where he grew up. He allowed me to record him telling known stories such as the tale of 'Rubh na Marbh', as well as his own memories of astonishing events from his childhood years on these now abandoned islands.

Mapping the Sea, a recent oral-history project by social ecologist Ruth Brennan and artist Stephen Hurrel, also demonstrates the continuing life of stories and traditions passed on by word of mouth. You can now listen online to Katie Douglas's lively telling of the story associated with a Barra place-name, located on a digital chart.

The transcriptions and especially the recordings reveal the unobtrusive, taut craft of artists in their own right. I never realised it at the time but I now know that my mother Johann Stephen (née Smith) and her sisters and brothers also had that way of telling a story. I think back to our council house rocking with laughter when my uncle John 'Bulldog' Smith, then schoolmaster at Sandwick, shared something he'd heard in the village. Kenny Murdo 'Safety' Smith told us tales of the Lewis bogeyman Mac an t-Sronaich, which I now know came down to him from his father, Murdo Finlay Smith, a legendary storyteller and debater in the village of Shawbost and the town of Stornoway.

My grandfather had a strong faith in education and was a keen reader, but he has also passed on the sheer pleasure he took in vernacular culture – songs, poems and stories. All his family seemed to retain respect for that culture even though several went on to become distinguished academics.

There is a telling comparison between the arts of the oral story and that of the written short story in *Cowries and Kobos: The West African Oral Tale and Short Story*, edited by Kirsten Holst-Petersen and Anna Rutherford, from my own first publishers, Dangaroo Press, Denmark. I wish I could quote Donald Consentino's introduction in full, but this sentence is telling: 'The fact that the oral narrative (folktale) and the short written narrative (short story) represent closed artistic systems is important to recognise, if only because critics so often miss the perfection of form that each of the narrative types has achieved.'

Most readers will be aware of the Hebridean fascination with stories linked to death and tragedy. The late singer Ishbel MacAskill often joked about this, between heart-rending renditions of our anthems. But the very wit she used to describe them is a sign of another less well-known strand of storytelling in the Outer Hebrides. Many tales depend on wordplay and wit and are thus impossible to deliver in another language. Angus Duncan's memories of Scarp in *Hebridean Island* and Kenneth MacDonald's *Peat Fire Memories* (both from Tuckwell Press) catch the way everyday yarns and banter alternate with tales of profound psychological depth. R.M. MacIver, one of the many Hebrideans who moved away to an international academic career, also catches the vitality of a storytelling culture in the very title of his autobiography, *As A Tale That Is Told* (University of Chicago Press). The point is confirmed by the folklorist Dr Margaret Bennett, recording Donald MacLennan as he recalled witty tales from Lewis still told by the descendants of emigrants to Quebec.*

These tales are for telling. There is copyright on the written form, developed by one individual author, but there is no copyright on the tale itself. I think you have to become immersed in a story till you are secure in a sense of its backbone structure. Then you can be yourself when you tell it. In one sense it is in your own voice and in another you've become lost in the telling. This book will be well worthwhile if readers enjoy stories they might not have encountered. It will be even more worthwhile if they are then passed on to someone else.

*(*Tocher* no. 52, 1996, School of Scottish Studies, University of Edinburgh.)

Appendix

The Western Isles are often associated with the Callanish Stones, on Lewis. I don't tell any stories linked directly to that astonishing feat of engineering – a story in itself. But one of the best stories I know is set at the farm at Callanish. It was transcribed by Donald Morrison, whose collecting preserved many of the tales gathered here. I am grateful to Western Isles Libraries, Creative Scotland and Shetland Arts for the Reader in Residence post at Western Isles Libraries, 2011–12, which enabled me to become immersed in that collection and in other recorded folk tales from the Western Isles. With kind permission, the transcribed text from the original manuscript is reproduced here. The tale is dated at around 1700.

The Clever Grieve

About the beginning of the last century, a certain farmer whom they called MacKorr held the farm at Callanish in Lewis. I do not suppose that he was originally a native of the islands. He sometimes went across to the mainland to sell cows and horses and on one of those visits he met a young man at a fair who told him that he was looking for a job.

MacKorr needed someone to manage his farm and he asked this young man if he would enter his employment. The young man agreed. 'What are you good for?' enquired McKorr.

Replied the man, 'I am good for three different vocations, namely:

I am good for sleeping long in a storm.
I am good at keeping bairns from the fire.
I am good at gathering friends to a feast.

'Well,' replied MacKorr. 'No person will take you as his grieve if you do not give a better account of yourself.'

'Tis no matter. If you take the chance of my service a little time will explain to you that what I said concerning the different things I am good for will be discovered by you and will satisfy you as to the truth of what I said.'

So they came to an agreement and the young man came with MacKorr to Lewis.

The first labouring season came and at the usual time all MacKorr's neighbours began to plough and to sow the seed. But MacKorr's grieve, although he ploughed the ground, would not yet sow any seed in it. Days passed and still he did not sow but one day, when he found the temperature of the earth to be right, he sowed the oats and the barley. The next big job was the cutting of the peats and the grieve took a novel way in doing this also, in the cutting of them and in the preserving of them when they were seasoned and ready to be stacked.

The return that MacKorr got from his crops that year was a matter of much talk among the neighbouring farmers, after it had been gathered into the corn yard to be stacked. After the barley and oat crop had been secured, the next task was to thatch MacKorr's houses and the superintendence of this work was also given to the grieve. The houses were thatched and roped more securely than ever before; likewise the corn stacks in the corn yard were roped so very securely that neither storm nor drift would part a rope from them.

Now the new crop of peats was begun to be used and the grieve put on the first fire with these new peats. And as soon as this fire yielded its heat and warmth, no bairns or grown men or women would go near it, because it was so hot.

Now said the grieve to his master: 'Now you see that I am good at keeping bairns at a distance from the fire.'

'I see that,' replied MacKorr.

Shortly after this there came a great storm one night, by which MacKorr's neighbours suffered very much. The storm took the thatch from some of their houses and swept away some of their corn stacks, so that they were kept busy through the night and the following morning. Yet for all their trouble and wit in saving their property from the ravages of this storm all of them sustained a loss, both of corn and houses, even roofs blowing away.

MacKorr himself was awakened by the tremendous noise of the storm and got out of bed, no doubt thinking that his property would be damaged like that of the others. He stayed up all that night and the following morning, looking about his property – but both his corn stacks and his house stood firm. Not so much as a single rope came off either house or stack.

When MacKorr saw that he was safe from the ravages of the storm and the tempest abated, he went into his house, where his grieve, late as it was, was still sleeping very easy in his bed. MacKorr went to his bedside and said to him, 'Oh man, you sleep too long this morning, with our poor neighbours keeping watch both night and day, but, after all, they have lost materially by the tempest, both in crops and houses.'

The grieve replied: 'Have you suffered like them?'

'No, my property is safe. But I was wondering that you were so careless as not to rise out of your bed on hearing this hurricane.'

'Why, master, did I not tell you that I was good for sleeping in a storm?' And he went on: 'And now you see that I might sleep regardless of the storm, as for all its fury, it could not injure either your corn nor houses. And that is owing to the precautions I took in securing both your corn and houses in the proper way and season. And such as do not will inevitably suffer such loss as the losses of your neighbours may reveal to you.'

MacKorr thus knew that two of the grieve's claims of his abilities had now been proved. There remained the third – 'gathering friends to a feast'.

At Christmas that year, MacKorr was so overjoyed at the improvement in his crops and the security of his property as to ask his grieve to go away on the following day and give general notice to all his friends to come to Callanish and spend Christmas with him. The grieve asked his master how far he should go.

'Reach the River at Barvas and then return home.'

The grieve went off and travelled until he reached the Barvas river. There he turned back and cried out at each of the farms as he passed them – not what MacKorr had told him but this.

He cried out in a sorrowful way that all MacKorr's houses had taken fire; that the fire had devoured all the thatch upon the houses; that as MacKorr suffered all this, he sent notice to all his friends on that side of the island to come to Callanish and bring a bundle of straw each to him. To thatch his houses afresh. That he sent notice to his friends of his misfortune and that he hoped they would not forget him in his adversity. The grieve cried the above through the farms, but of all the tenants in that place only five arrived at Callanish the next day, with a bundle of straw on the back of each.

When MacKorr saw the bundles of straw he asked what did this mean? The grieve then told MacKorr what he had told these friends – and that he had indeed warned all whom MacKorr called his friends all along that coast. But when he had told them of MacKorr's loss those 'friends' had stayed away. He went on: 'But these five persons now come to your house are all the true friends you have on that coast. Show them now that you are their friend, for I consider them worthy of your regard and confidence.'

MacKorr, learning how the grieve had counterfeited his message in order to find out his real friends for him upon that coast, thanked the grieve both for his good sense and penetration. MacKorr thus spent the Christmas with those true friends indeed and the third of the grieve's capabilities was thus proved.